SPARKS FLY

PHOENIX RIDGE FIRE DEPARTMENT

EMILY HAYES

1

HALLIE

"I'm just saying, when you start counting, the math starts to seem a little pathetic. You want to know how many people I've pulled from burning buildings?"

Lieutenant Hallie Hunter is trying not to choke on her coffee through barely contained laughter. She leans against the countertop in the break room at Fire Station 3, in the bustling resort city of Mesquite, Nevada. Her colleague and friend, Arthur Byrne, seems to be struggling through a midlife crisis in his career this morning.

"Go on then, Art. How many people have you saved from burning buildings?"

"Twenty-seven. Can you believe that? Thirty-five years at the station and I'm not even averaging one a year. Now ask me how many cats I've saved. Go on! Ask me."

Hallie has to reluctantly put her coffee down; the choking risk is becoming too great.

"How many cats?"

"Ninety-fucking-three. Ninety-three cats, Hallie! Stuck up trees, on roofs, under porches. I've been a shining knight in armor to nearly a hundred of the damned furballs. I don't even like cats!"

Hallie's grin is starting to make her face hurt as she chuckles again.

"Hey now, I won't hear any cat slander in my presence, cats are the best. Call me a lesbian cliché, I don't care." She holds up both her hands as Art joins her in laughing warmly. "But I see your point, you never picture as a rookie that you'll spend way more time at the top of a ladder waving cold cuts than parading heroically out of a raging inferno."

"Exactly! Don't get me wrong, I'm glad for it now. We've both seen enough horror in our years to appreciate the boring call-outs. It just hits me every year when the new recruits are due, they have no idea they'll be sitting with a coffee in thirty-odd years, counting how many cats owe them one of their nine lives."

Hallie smirks and nods, picking her coffee back up and silently thanking the stars for the quiet days. Before she can take another sip, Captain Hewitt leans round the doorframe.

"Hunter, my office if you will." He is strolling off as quickly as he appeared.

Art raises his eyebrows as Hallie wonders what could possibly have warranted the rare invitation. A gurgling sort of apprehension takes up residence in her stomach as she dares to consider that maybe, just maybe, he wants to discuss the promotion she's been grinding so hard for. This district has never seen a female fire captain. Hell, they'd never seen a female lieutenant before Hallie Hunter. She'd managed to claw her way up the ladder by tooth and nail, the weight of incessant male prejudice threatening to break her ankles the entire time.

Hallie would never tell a soul, but it's been her birthday wish for more than a decade to make captain by forty. Just a few weeks on from her thirty-ninth birthday, she's hoping beyond hope that today could be the day. Chugging the last dregs of her lukewarm coffee, she spares Art an affectionate clap on the shoulder on her way out.

"Happy Monday, old man. Now go save a bunny or something."

Hallie strolls into the captain's office with an easy smile but it falters slightly when she sees who's already occupying the second chair in front of the desk.

"Morning, Sir. Barker." She nods to the captain and then to the only other lieutenant in the station, that excited flutter in her stomach instantly curdling like sour milk. If she's about to be told Jeff Barker is being promoted above her, despite being five years younger than her and a total dick, Hallie will lose her mind. Give her a few bottles of wine and let her cats try and eat her when she passes out. She's sure that sounds like more fun that swallowing Barker's boasting about outranking her.

"Hunter, have a seat. Barker is about to make your day."

Hallie's eyebrows disappear into the flaxen curls which always flop onto her forehead when they're not secured beneath a helmet or a baseball cap. She takes a seat, unsure how to feel as the captain looks at Jeff expectantly.

"Right, yeah, Hallie, I'm sure you're gonna be pleased about this but try not to throw a party just yet. I'm leaving at the end of the month."

"I, um, I'm sorry?" She shifts in her seat uncomfortably, unsure if she just walked into a dismissal, completely oblivious. As far as she knew, Jeff hadn't done anything even remotely worth being fired for—not unless you count being a cocky bastard every day of the week. She glances to the captain, even more confused by the encouraging smile he's giving her. Surely, he doesn't expect her to celebrate right in front of Jeff's face.

"Barker is leaving us for a teaching role at the Academy. So," he claps his hands together, "I need you to take over Probationary Field Training for the new recruits. We have eight incoming next Monday."

It takes every ounce of stoic control in Hallie's body not to leap out of her chair and whoop. Leading PFT is exactly the step up she needs on her mission to make captain. She still shudders at the memory of the wine hangover from the day after Jeff snagged the position three years ago. Pasting on a more calmly grateful expression, she responds.

"Absolutely, Sir. Happy to take on the challenge." Turning to Jeff—who she suddenly hates much less—she tries to sound innocently curious when she asks, "What's got you abandoning us for the Academy then, Barker? Desk job doesn't sound like your style."

Jeff snorts, probably seeing right through Hallie's subtle interrogation. They've been at each other's throats for almost ten years. Hallie can't think of any reason good enough for Jeff to abandon their ruthless race to the top.

"Jenny and I are expecting our first kiddo. She wants me doing something boring and safe, so she doesn't have to worry about me leaving for a shift I don't come home from."

"Oh, well congratulations are in order then."

This time Jeff's snort becomes a full-on guffaw, as if Hallie had just stuck on a clown nose and offered him a diaper-shaped balloon.

"Appreciate the well wishes, I guess, but be honest, I know you think I'm insane. Pigs will fly before Hallie Hunter gives up her shot at chief some day for a mundane suburban family life."

The captain adds his muted chuckle into the mix, and Hallie tries her best to act equally amused. He's right; in a way, nothing has ever mattered more to her than chasing her dreams as a firefighter and proving to every male pig in this field that she can do anything just as well as them, if not better. But Hallie can't ignore the little pang of loneliness that stabs at her lungs through the forced laughter.

She'd never said she didn't want a "suburban family life" at *some* point. A wife, kids, the whole nine yards. She's just never met the right woman. A woman who wouldn't ask her to give up the mission she's dedicated her entire adult life to, just because the job can be high risk. She needs someone who would understand what it means to her, someone who could see that leaving the action for a desk job would put out the fire behind her own eyes. So far, a woman like that has been hard to find. Jeff's wife is a case in point.

"Ah, you know me, Barker. I've got too many rookies to babysit to think about starting a crew of my own. I'm raising the next generation in my own way." Hallie adds a cheesy wink in the hopes she can convince both men that she's not the teeniest bit jealous of Jeff's cozy homelife. "Well, sounds like I've got a ton of new training exercises to map out. Lord knows Jeff here has been churning out a few softies lately. Will that be all, Captain?"

"Sure, Hunter. We'll coordinate later in the

week. Say Thursday? You can give me a rundown of your plans."

"Sounds good, Sir." Hallie offers him a final nod and tries not to let her smile creep too close to the smug side as she throws Jeff a mock salute on her way out.

Sprawled on the floor surrounded by endless sheets of badly scribbled blueprints, Hallie sips on her large glass of pinot noir. The day had slipped by without incident, not one distressed citizen with two legs or four, and she had spent it all dreaming up her own program to train the incoming rookies to her exact standards. She's going to produce the best crew this department has ever seen. They'll be the pride and joy of her career to date.

Hell, they'll be the pride and joy of my whole life to date.

Hallie drowns out the thought with another gulp of wine. She hadn't been prepared for the hollow disappointment the bare walls of her one-bedroom apartment had seemed to blanket her with the minute she'd walked through the door. Not even the enthusiastic greeting of her twin tabbies made her feel better; they were probably only winding their way round her ankles in the hopes of flirting for an early dinner. Try as she might, she hadn't been able to shake the image of Jeff chasing a bouncing toddler through the kids' park at the end of the street, a laughing Jenny watching them from a bench, swollen with baby number two. All of a sudden, Hallie's life was starting to look like the more *mundane* option. She'd immediately grabbed the bottle of red from the kitchen counter, half empty from the afternoon she'd spent soaking in the bath yesterday. The highlight of her entire weekend. Alone.

Scraping her fingers through the short hair at the back of her head, Hallie lets out a frustrated groan. This gloomy feeling is raining all over her Probationary Field Training parade, and she's sick of it. Draining the rest of her glass, she sits up to take an overview of her master plan. Focusing intently on clawing back the pride and satisfaction that had filled her to the brim in the captain's office this morning, she grabs her phone from the couch behind her and pulls up *Pop* in her contacts. It rings only twice before his joy-crinkled face fills the screen.

"Hey there, Hallie-Pallie. What's happening?"

Hallie inhales deeply as her shadowy mood brightens just a bit, a face-splitting grin bringing an ache to her cheeks while her father holds the phone mere inches from his bulbous nose.

"Hey, Pop. Not much, not much. Just planning the most epic PFT course in this station's history."

"Well now, isn't that a headline and a half! No doubt you'll whip those rookies into shape in no time. Tell me all about it."

They fall into an easy chatter, the squeeze in Hallie's chest easing with every new exercise she describes for her Pop's enthusiastic approval.

"Sheesh, Hallie. What a rodeo! I'm starting to think I'd never have made it through training if you were lieutenant back in my day."

"Ah, don't be ridiculous, Pop. I'm only throwing at them everything you ever taught me." Her chest fills with pride again, but this time not for herself. This gentle giant of a man beaming back at her, impossible to contain within the few inches of phone screen, is the sole reason she ever wanted to be a firefighter in the first place.

Andrew Hunter—Sandy to his nearest and dearest—is the retired chief of the Eureka County Fire Brigade, and Hallie's biggest hero. Growing up his only daughter, in a county populated by less than two thousand people, she'd always regarded Chief Hunter as something of a legend. Moving to a city ten times the size hadn't robbed her of that belief in the slightest.

Her gaze settles warmly on the family photo propped up on the shelf above her TV. There's Sandy, planting a sloppy kiss on the rosy cheek of Hallie's Ma, Marie, while her head is thrown back, mid-laugh. Then down in front there's little Hallie, wide grin revealing two missing teeth, and bright blonde pigtails being held above her head like bunny ears by her big brother, Gavin. It strikes her how weedy he looks, barely scraping thirteen, while thirty years later he's a captain in the raucous Las Vegas District. Two legacy firefighters, smiling like loons on a camping trip with their loved-up parents.

This time the wave of sadness crashes into Hallie faster than she can think to take a breath.

"Whoa there, Pallie. Where'd you go? You look like you've been eaten by a black cloud."

"Huh? Oh no, nothing, Pop. I'm all good. Just got a lot of work to do, you know? I'll let you go."

Hallie struggles to maintain eye contact with

her father's concerned frown, sure that he sees right through her hasty cover story. But he doesn't need to know she's wallowing in her own self-pity on the day she's supposed to be celebrating.

Not that he wouldn't understand.

Mom and Pop spent their twenties in Vegas, like Gavin chose to do a generation later. Pop, the fearless firefighter and Ma, the badass ER nurse. They only ended up moving back to Eureka because Pop's mom got sick, choosing to start their family once life had slowed right down.

Sure, Hallie knew if she shared her fears with them, that she'd missed her shot at the happy family life because she was too busy chasing the big career, they'd understand. But she isn't one for family therapy, and she couldn't bear to resent her parents even a tiny bit for seemingly having everything they've ever wanted in life. No, she clamps down on the emotions and forces a big grin, most likely a mere ghost of the one she'd shown when Pop first answered her call.

"Mm-kay, whatever you say. Don't work yourself to death, hon. We're here if you need us. Love you."

"Love you, Pop. Give a kiss to Mom for me. Speak soon."

She hangs up the phone and sits for a moment, still cross-legged on her living room floor, until the silence begins to close in again.

Screw it, I need another glass of wine.

2

KAIA

Kaia Montgomery smooths her navy-blue uniform one last time before walking through the automatic doors of Fire Station 3. Her heart is pounding as she takes in the spacious garage bay to her left, already bustling with activity. Firefighters in turnout gear are doing equipment checks, while others come and go through a door labelled *WATCH ROOM*. The enormous red engines lined up before the garage doors spark an excitement in her she hasn't felt since she snuck into her first R-rated movie.

This is really happening.

After twelve months spent qualifying as an EMT, and a further three at the Fire Academy, Kaia is more than ready to get stuck into the action.

Taking a moment to breathe it all in, she exhales all the doubts that have been piled on her since she first declared she wanted to become a firefighter. She's doing this for herself, and nothing and no one will get in her way.

"Montgomery! Over here, let's go!" a gruff voice calls out.

Kaia straightens her spine and strides toward the assembly room, where seven other recruits in matching uniforms are lounging against rows of desks. She can't stop the small smirk from playing on her lips as she realizes she's the only woman in the group. Just like she was often the only girl getting detained back in high school for pulling stunts like climbing up the roof to spray-paint profanities, Kaia is no stranger to running with the guys. She only wonders if they'll embrace her like her two older brothers and their schoolyard gangs or if they'll sneer at her, the weak chick in the testosterone chain.

The door bangs open and a striking, muscular woman strides into the room, chin held high, eyes alight with an intensity that makes Kaia's breath catch. She cuts an impressive figure in her immaculately creased uniform, short blonde hair curling wildly atop her head but shaved at the back and sides. Kaia resists the urge to bite her lip, surrounded on all sides by stacked dudes in their mid- to late-twenties, there's only one person commanding her attention.

Well, hello there, Muscle Mommy.

"Recruits, welcome to Fire Station 3," she says, her authoritative tone slicing through the dwindling conversations throughout the room. "I'm Lieutenant Hunter, your commanding officer for Probationary Field Training over the next eighteen months."

Her piercing blue stare sweeps over each of them appraisingly before settling on Kaia with a hint of surprise. Kaia holds the lieutenant's gaze, a spark of challenge flickering behind her own brown eyes.

Hunter's jaw tightens almost imperceptibly before she continues. "I have to admit, I'm a little disappointed at this ongoing gender inequity in our ranks. You'd think by 2024 we'd have more than just one female recruit."

She lets out a soft, disappointed scoff, shaking her head. Kaia feels her cheeks flush, immediately feeling the eyes of every other recruit burning into the side of her face. At the sound of a few barely contained sniggers, she squares her shoulders and sits up a little straighter. She's used to being under-estimated and dismissed by men—their fragile egos always threatened by a confident woman who won't be cowed. But locking eyes with the woman she's decided will be her ally, her champion in this old boys' club... the muttered remarks that she should *go make a sandwich* only stoke Kaia's smoldering determination.

"If you want to last a minute in this station, you can shut your traps. I can assure you; I have zero tolerance for discrimination or harassment of any kind," Hunter goes on, fixing them all with a stern glare. "We're firefighters first, entrusted with protecting lives regardless of race, gender, or identity. If any of you can't check your egos and treat Montgomery with the same respect as her male counterparts, you'll find yourself out of this program before you can say *backdraft*."

She punctuates her declaration by assessing each of the men in turn, her icy eyes daring them to so much as cough. Kaia swallows hard, terribly aware of their dismissive sidelong glances in response to the lieutenant's warning.

This is going to be one hell of an uphill battle.

What else is new? Kaia is no stranger to having to prove herself. If she hadn't learned to rough and tumble with the best of them, her older brothers would no doubt have left her in the dust growing up while throwing out insults about Barbie dolls and tea parties. But they couldn't help their prejudices, they were drilled into them from birth. If her parents hadn't divorced before she'd finished kindergarten, Kaia is sure her father would have crushed her bold spirit with his archaic views on how a girl should behave.

Sure, he loved her, but he'd probably love her more if she were quieter, more respectful, more interested in settling down and learning to cook something other than scrambled eggs. The grumpy ex-cop still firmly believes she should leave the dangerous jobs to the men. He certainly never recruited any women in his own department all those years. Well, she'll show these arrogant pricks the same thing she intends to show her dad —that she's stronger, smarter, and more fearless than any of them.

Kaia lifts her chin and matches Hallie's piercing stare with one of grim determination. Screw fragile male egos. She's got this. And she'll have the last laugh when she emerges at the top of this graduating class, showing this fiery lieutenant she can be a worthy contender for Head Bitch in

Charge. With every sentence of Hunter's ongoing speech, Kaia feels more and more sure that this fearsome woman is going to shape her into the best version of herself she can be.

"Let's get one thing straight. I have been a fire-fighter for nearly twenty years. Embedded with the LAFD during their worst wildfire season, rappelled off a crumbling skyscraper in Vegas, even joined extrication teams for rescue missions in our very own Desert Valley. You'd be hard pressed to find another lieutenant in this district with my record, and I did it all without a penis dangling between my legs."

Kaia's breath catches in her throat as Hallie starts stalking slowly down the line of men, heels clacking against the scuffed assembly room floor. Hunter's full lips are curved in the faintest hint of a sneer, daring any of them to challenge her position as their trainer.

"I have earned every single one of my acco-lades, medals, and promotions by being the most capable, quick-thinking firefighter on every scene I've worked," Hallie growls. "If any of you Runt Recruits has a problem taking orders from a woman with ten times the experience and creden-tials as your entire class combined... well, I'd suggest picking a new career field. Because I'll burn you so fast your matchstick dicks will be ash before you can even bitch about it."

A ringing silence falls over the assembly room. Kaia can almost hear her own thundering heart-beat as Hunter stops right in front of her, those scorching blue flame eyes dancing over Kaia's face as if daring *her*, right alongside the rest of them, to doubt a woman's worth in this line of work. Despite herself, Kaia feels her lips twitching with the urge to smirk, to push this lioness of a woman even further to parade her strength.

Hunter's eyes narrow to mere slits as she holds Kaia's gaze in a heated standoff. The tension stretches so taut, Kaia is certain someone could strike a match off it. Then, just as abruptly as the heated silence descended, the lieutenant tears her eyes away with a contemptuous snort.

"Change into your PT gear and report to the training yard. We'll start weeding out which of you sad sacks actually has what it takes." With that final command launched, she spins on her heel and stalks toward the door.

Kaia is the last to break from her stupor, the cottony scent of Hunter's crisp uniform mixed with a faint, musky cologne seeming to linger in the air.

She has to gulp down a harsh breath, cracking her neck just to snap herself into movement, as a sudden throbbing ache blossoms between her thighs.

Sweet Jesus, am I turned on right now? Were we just checking each other out?

No, that can't be it. Kaia has just never encountered a woman quite like Lieutenant Hunter before in her life. That whirlwind of blistering confidence and intense prowess and complete control over every person and situation surrounding her. That sense of powerful dominance cloaking Hunter's every movement and utterance like a rich, intoxicating perfume...

Kaia shakes her head sharply, trying to dislodge the dizzying fog of attraction. She needs to focus, to keep her head in the game if she hopes to have any chance at proving herself here. Wrangling her raging hormones and this alarming hunger to impress their fiery lieutenant is simply not an option right now.

Even so, she can't quite stifle the tingling thrill skating up her spine as she follows her fellow rookies out to the training yard, the rest of them parting like schoolboys to allow their imposing commander space. Yeah, this dynamic is unlike anything Kaia has ever had the pleasure of witnessing. But as she watches the lithe, powerful lines of Hunter's body flow through some warm-up stretches, she can't deny that she's already becoming an absolute addict for it.

"Recruits! Line it up!" Hunter's commanding bark slices through the humid morning air.

The eight of them quickly scramble into formation, Kaia wincing as the buckles on her gear dig into her skin. The lieutenant stalks down the line again, that scorching appraisal seeming to sear right through each of them.

"We start conditioning with sprints in full turnout gear plus breathing apparatus packs," she announces curtly. "Anything less than your full effort will be immediately obvious to me and repaid with extra repetitions after. Am I making myself unmistakably clear?"

A ragged chorus of "Yes, Lieutenant!" answers her. Kaia focuses on the tiny bead of sweat trailing slowly down the firmly lean column of Hunter's throat, forcing her mind to remain laser-sharp rather than wandering elsewhere.

"Then what are you mouth-breathers still standing around for? Let's move!"

With that, they're off. Kaia's calves and lungs

are already burning within a few dozen yards, the unforgiving Nevada sun beating down from above. She can hear the rasping breaths of the men around her, taste the sour tang of their struggle and exertion. A small, vicious thrill races through her veins.

This is her element—pushing her physical limits while chasing that euphoric edge of pain and pure power. Ignoring the protesting aches in her limbs, Kaia digs deeper and starts pumping her arms with renewed vigor. One by one, she tears past the floundering recruits until she's dead even with the lead man.

Risking a sidelong glance, Kaia's lips curl in a silent snarl as she catches his shocked, narrowed eyes. He's likely not used to having a woman shove past and outpace him so easily. Good. Kaia lives for cracking that fragile male ego wide open.

At the end of the first lap, Hunter's sharp whistle pierces the air. As the recruits trip over themselves grinding to a gasping halt, Kaia keeps her longer stride going right past the starting line. She can practically feel the weight of Hunter's laser-focused stare singeing the back of her sweaty shirt.

Only once she's put an extra fifteen yards

between herself and the men does Kaia finally spin and rejoin the lineup. Chest heaving, she throws her arms over her head and stretches lazily, very aware of the venomous looks being thrown her way.

"Just getting a little head start, Lieutenant," she rasps with a cheeky wink.

Rather than the scathing reprimand Kaia expects, Hunter's full lips twitch in what might actually be amusement. A teasing glint dances in those arctic irises for the barest hint of a second.

"How generous of you to do extra credit from the jump, Montgomery," she drawls. Her gaze rakes over Kaia from head to toe in a scorching appraisal. "Though surviving my training program relies on staying upright until I'm satisfied you've shown me everything you've got. Is that a challenge you think you can meet?"

Kaia's pulse hammers in her ears as realization sparks—this intense drill, with its impossible demands—it's a freaking mind game Hunter is playing. Trying to weed out who will be the first to crack under the strain, whether through physical failing or mental weakness. A delicious shiver races up Kaia's spine at the thought of squaring off against such a merciless adversary.

There's only one possible response.

"Always, Lieutenant," Kaia husks, holding Hunter's expectant stare as a bead of sweat trails slowly between her breasts. "I never disappoint."

This time, Hunter's slight smirk is unmistakable before she blows a shrill burst on her whistle to signal another lap.

From there, the morning fitness circuit becomes a blistering gauntlet of one-upmanship. Whenever one of the other recruits starts to fade or let their form slip, Kaia seizes the moment to surge ahead with obnoxious showboating— adding extra overhead presses to her fireman carries, doing diving push-up burpees between laps. Her muscles sing with every confident repetition, squashing any doubts she can't pack on the protein like the rest of them.

More than once, one of the winded men hurls a nasty insult or profane slur at her preening efforts. But Kaia only drinks in their frothing rage with a smug grin, spurred on by the electric tingle of Hunter's approving gaze tracking her every arrogant move.

It's towards the end of an especially grueling set—weighted lunges combined with high knees

—that Kaia's distracted performance finally earns her a rebuke.

"Montgomery! What in the hell do you think you're doing?" Hunter's sharp yell cuts through Kaia's panting exertion like a slap. "Are you actually attempting those tire jumps with your laces untied? Do you have a death wish?"

Kaia halts mid stride, chest heaving as she follows Hunter's incredulous scowl down to her flopping bootlaces. Shit, she hadn't even realized.

"There's no excuse to get sloppy," Hunter growls, suddenly right in Kaia's face with those blazing blues boring into her. Kaia's mouth goes unbearably dry as the heat of Hunter's words gusts across her slick skin. "If you were to trip face-first at a live scene, your untied hazard could cost a life —be it yours, a civilian's, or one of your own crewmate's who has to compensate for your reckless mistake."

The naked disappointment and accusation in Hunter's tone hits Kaia like a bucket of icy water, extinguishing the giddy high of her gratuitous antics. The lieutenant steps back, eyes flaying Kaia where she stands, before she addresses the group.

"You may call me a stickler for presentation and protocol, but this job demands absolute focus and discipline at all times, not just when it's convenient for your swollen egos," Hunter's scathing rebuke slices through the tense silence. "If you aren't prepared to make that commitment, you have no business calling yourselves firefighters. We'll pick this up again after lunch with some team-building exercises to remind you of what this uniform represents."

With that, she turns on her heel and stalks off, seemingly oblivious to the way Kaia remains rooted in place.

Who is this woman? And why do I want her so much?

3

HALLIE

"Let's go, go, go! Time is lives, people!"

Hallie's barked orders echo through the burn building as she ushers the rookie class into position. Thick plumes of machine-generated smoke billow around them, the harsh tang of acridity coating the back of her throat.

"Scenario is this: We have multiple civilians trapped on the upper floors. Entry team will advance the hose line while rescue teams move to extract. Maintain your spacing and communication at all times. First team, ready?"

A ragged chorus of "Ready, Lieutenant!" responds and Hallie gives a curt nod to the observation instructor running the drill. With a deafening blast of the electronic fire simulations, chaos erupts around them.

"Go, go, go!" Hallie shouts over the roar as the first squad charge in. She watches with a critical eye as they fumble their way into a sloppy line advancement, the hose team already breaking formation.

"Too wide, Cochran! You'll never get that hose around the corner! Nguyen, verbal all clear before you—"

A fresh cloud of smoke erupts, swallowing the stumbling recruits in a churning maelstrom. Hallie grits her teeth, fighting the urge to jump in and correct their piss-poor form herself, when she catches a flicker of movement through the haze.

Of course. Montgomery, breaching way too far ahead of her team. Again.

"Montgomery!" Hallie's bellow cuts through the cacophony like a whipcrack. "Get back, now! You don't leave until I give the order!"

She can barely make out Kaia's silhouette pausing, that stubborn streak already shining through in her body language. A few tense seconds tick by...and then, finally, the reckless recruit falls back into line with her squad.

"Goddammit," Hallie snarls under her breath.

How many times will she have to drill this into Kaia's overeager head? You never, ever leave your team behind. Rookie arrogance like that is gonna get someone killed one of these days. She watches the rest of the drill beneath furrowed brows, a dull headache quickly forming from the strain.

"Montgomery, front and center! Now!"

Hallie barely waits until the smoke has cleared from the burn room before unleashing her fury. The rest of the recruits are still catching their breath, rips and soot stains marring their turnouts. All except for Kaia Montgomery, of course. She strides right up with that stupidly confident gait, not a single flicker of shame on her effortlessly beautiful features.

"The hell was that in there?" Hallie demands, crowding into Kaia's space until they are practically nose-to-nose. She can feel the heat radiating off the younger woman's skin in waves. "You disobeying direct orders just for kicks? Or are you actually trying to get this whole unit killed?"

Up close, Hallie can see the bead of sweat tracing an irresistible path along Kaia's sculpted cheekbone. The slight hitch in her chest as Hallie's breath mingles with her own. For a defiant moment, their heated gazes remain locked in a battle of wills.

Then Kaia's full lips part with a soft huff of air. "I had it handled," she murmurs, seemingly unaffected by Hallie looming over her.

A little thrill sparks in Hallie's gut at that blatant insubordination. She bites back the desire to grab Kaia by the collar of that sweat-damp uniform and really let her have it. Instead, she leans even closer until their noses are nearly brushing.

"You arrogant jackass," Hallie growls in a tone that dares Kaia to so much as blink first. "Next time I say stay in formation, you stay in formation. Or so help me, Montgomery, you'll be running drill cones until your legs give out from under you. Are we clear?"

Kaia stares right back at her, those rich brown eyes swirling with a storm of rebelliousness and something else Hallie can't quite put her finger on. Hallie feels her heart kick up another beat, drowning out the sounds of the other recruits shuffling awkwardly around them.

Then, slowly, Kaia gives a minute nod. "Crystal, Lieutenant."

For a suspended moment, they are the only two people in the world.

"Hit the showers, all of you. Come back better tomorrow or there will be hell to pay."

Hallie marches back to her office without sparing the rest of the recruits a second glance. She couldn't bear to read on any of their faces what they made of the heated exchange. Most likely they enjoyed seeing Kaia receive a dressing down, and that makes Hallie sick to her stomach. She wants nothing more than for them to respect Kaia Montgomery as a fellow crewmate, to acknowledge her abilities instead of writing her off just for being female. But Kaia isn't doing herself any favors insisting on striking out alone. They're all as bad as each other, and Hallie has to somehow forge an indestructible machine out of their resistant parts.

She blows out a harsh breath as she sags back in her desk chair, suddenly feeling every one of her thirty-nine years. She squeezes her eyes shut and tries to block out the memory of Kaia's face mere inches from her own. Those impossibly full lips so close she could have leaned in to—

No. Absolutely not.

Hallie snaps her lids open with a sharp shake of her head. Getting carried away with inappropriate bullshit like that would be career-ending faster than she could blink. Sure, Kaia's dogged determination is impressive as hell, and that fearless swagger of hers is even more captivating up close. But none of that gives Hallie any excuse to be undressing the cock-sure little rookie with her eyes.

"Keep it professional, Hunter," she berates herself in a fierce mutter. "Montgomery's just another pain-in-the-ass kid who still hasn't learned how to follow a goddamn order around here."

Hallie forces herself to review the rest of the recruits' sloppy performances from the last drill, anything to scrub Kaia's teasing glare from her mind's eye. The open defiance and that maddening spark of want she could have sworn she'd seen flickering there for an instant. It had to have been her tired, over-worked brain playing tricks, nothing more.

Just an arrogant ass who needs to be bent over your knee.

The unbidden thought whispers through

Hallie's subconscious. Her traitorous libido help-
fully painting a vivid fantasy of doing just that—
stripping away that smoky uniform until Kaia is
bare, then pulling those lean, muscular limbs over
her lap to—

"Jesus!" Hallie hisses through her teeth. Her
whole body pulsing with an electric jolt of pure
need, shocking her out of that wildly inappropriate train of thought. "Get it together," she orders
herself firmly. "That girl is completely off limits.
End of story."

Through the days that follow, Hallie dials up the
intensity for their outdoor training session,
pushing the recruits through a merciless rotation
of skills and drills. Hose bundling, hose line
advancement, Rescue Randy carries, ladder raises
—she cycles them through it all relentlessly with
only a few minutes' break between each fresh hell.
Anything to keep their bodies moving and minds
occupied rather than dwelling on the simmering
tension in the air.

Because no matter where Hallie positioned

herself on the training grounds, she could feel the heated energy rolling off of Kaia in thick, intoxicating currents. Even surrounded by her grumbling, stumbling squad mates, the strutting young firefighter moves with the same primal, effortless power as a panther slinking through the underbrush.

"C'mon, Cochran, are you serious right now?" Hallie can't resist sneering as the winded recruit struggles to heft his bundled hose over his shoulder. "If a woman half your size can kick your ass that easily..."

She jerks her head to where Kaia is casually flipping her lead-filled bundle into the air and back down again with each prowling step she takes. A thin sheen of sweat glistens on her skin and Hallie has to force herself to quickly look away.

"Then it's just embarrassing for the rest of you," she finishes, allowing the barest hint of a smirk to twist her lips as she can't fight the temptation to meet Kaia's molten gaze. The glistening recruit gives an infinitesimal nod of acknowledgement, like they are two alpha predators communicating in some silent, ancient language. Then she lurches back into her steady advancing, pausing by Cochran to swipe his hose from his sagging shoulders, and continuing across the yard with double the load.

That alone makes Hallie's gut clench and body thrum with awareness. God, she really needs this relentless onslaught of drills to come to an end soon. The front row seat to Kaia's brazen performance is becoming too distracting. Hallie lets herself believe for a moment that it might be more for her than the band of grumbling males. But the venomous muttering of snide remarks from Cochran and his crewmates snaps Hallie's awareness back to the task at hand. As much as Kaia's power lures her in, she needs the rookies to be a team. All of them.

"Montgomery, you're gonna run three full laps for that little show-pony stunt! Let's move!"

There. Hallie swallows hard as she watches Kaia respond instantly to the barked order, dropping her effortless rhythm to toe the line and take off at a ground-eating lope. If she has to keep piling on the discipline, no matter how arbitrary, to keep that sizzling current of attraction from growing into a raging fire...so be it.

Finally done with the hours of brutal training,

Hallie stands under the lukewarm stream of water in her locker room shower, letting it sluice over her aching muscles. She rolls her shoulders, trying to release some of the knots of tension that had taken up permanent residence there. For today's training session she had been ruthless, even more so than usual. But it seemed to be the only way to keep her raging thoughts from spiraling out into the wildly inappropriate whenever a certain cocky rookie was around.

"Lieutenant?"

The single, softly spoken word very nearly makes Hallie jump out of her skin. She spins with a violent splatter of water, mouth dropping open in surprise. There stands Kaia in just a sports bra and compression shorts, filling the doorway to the showers with her powerful frame.

"Montgomery!" Hallie sputters, instinctively crossing her arms over her bare breasts even as her eyes drank in those glistening ab muscles. "What are you—what do you want?"

Rather than looking chastised, Kaia merely arches an eyebrow in clear amusement. The smug little grin playing over those full lips makes the thundering of Hallie's pulse echo in her ears.

"Well, you made me run so many extra laps

today," Kaia drawls, "obviously I need a nice, long shower."

Hallie feels a creeping blush mar her cheeks as she grabs her towel to cover her dripping skin. So accustomed to having this locker room to herself, she'd completely forgotten that, of course, Kaia would be using the women's showers. Hallie's mouth goes impossibly dry as Kaia's dark eyes roam overtly over her barely concealed body. The younger woman doesn't even try to make her open appraisal a secret as she starts to slowly close the distance between them.

"Wh-what in the hell do you think you're doing, Montgomery?" Hallie's voice comes out a strangled rasp. She can't seem to decide whether she wants to maintain her glare or keep drinking in Kaia's own exposed curves that draw her gaze like a magnet.

"I just wanted to thank you for hyping me up in front of the guys today. I appreciate the support more than you know," Kaia murmurs silkily. She is nearly within arm's reach now, close enough for Hallie's skin to prickle with apprehension. The rookie lifts her chin in that stubborn, challenging way, pinning Hallie with that signature smoldering stare she was coming to crave.

Hallie's throat bobs as she swallows hard. She can actually smell the warm, earthy aroma of Kaia's skin overpowering the chemical tang of the locker room now. Feel the exquisite tension thrumming between their bodies in the humid air like a live current sparking at her nerve endings.

The truth is, Hallie wanted nothing more than to grab Kaia and slam her against those steamy tiles.

"Don't even think about it."

The sudden razor's edge in Hallie's tone makes Kaia freeze in place, tantalizingly close but not yet breaching the lieutenant's personal space. Hallie can see that playful glint in her dark, hooded eyes shutter instantly at the blatant warning.

Hallie marshals every ounce of her authority and willpower into a tone that would allow zero space for misinterpretation.

"We're going to go our separate ways. You're going to shower off, then report for equipment inspection before the end of day notes. And we'll both pretend like you didn't just barge in here looking for...whatever fresh hell that was supposed to be, understood?"

Kaia's jaw tightens, that stubborn line forming between her eyebrows like she's gearing up to argue. But Hallie has been pushed entirely too far already. She closes what little space remains between them with an authoritative step, putting them nose-to-nose as she glares up into those churning, brown depths.

"I'm serious, Montgomery," Hallie growls. "You do not want to fuck around and find out. This shit? Stops here and now before we both end up regretting it for the rest of our careers. Are we crystal-goddamn-clear?"

For an endless moment, they stay locked in that heated stand-off, the air between them practically sizzling with unreleased tension. Hallie watches a series of flickering micro-expressions chase themselves across Kaia's breathtaking features. Surprise. Hurt. Indignation. And something rawer that Hallie won't dare let herself name, for both their sakes.

Then Kaia lets out a soft huff through her nose, her dark eyes glinting with obvious disappointment. She takes one slow step back, re-establishing the appropriate space between her scantily clad chest and Hallie's own racing heart.

"Understood," she mutters, her deep voice gone husky. They hold each other's stare for another few fraught seconds. Then Kaia turns on her heel and marches from the showers with powerful, ground-eating strides.

Hallie closes her eyes, letting out the harsh breath she hadn't realized she'd been holding. That was one bullet successfully dodged...for now.

4

KAIA

Equipment inspection passes in tense silence. For once, Kaia makes no attempt to stand out from the crowd. Still simmering in the embarrassment of Hunter's rejection, she makes her way through the various checks laser-focused. She doesn't bother to point out any of the other rookies' mistakes, just minds her own business in her desperation to be finished as quickly as possible.

"Hunter! Montgomery! My office, now."

Captain Hewitt's gruff bark rings out across the garage bay, instantly setting Kaia's heart pounding. She tears her gaze away from the row of breathing apparatus she'd been counting for the third time, a familiar knot of dread forming in her gut. She was called into the principal's office enough times in high school to know a warning tone when she heard one. Kaia spares a nervous glance at Hunter, who looks up sharply from her clipboard. Their eyes meet for the briefest charged instant before Hunter gives a quick nod.

"Make quick about it, Montgomery," she murmurs, already striding after the captain with that confident military gait. "The rest of you, get out of here, we're done for today."

Kaia swallows hard, trying to ignore the weight of the speculative stares of the other recruits as she trails after Hunter's purposeful strides. With every step, unbidden doubt bubbles up from her stomach—had she crossed the line with her antics in training? Or worse, had Hunter reported her misguided flirtation from the locker room straight after she had fled the scene?

I was just being stupid. Surely, she wouldn't rat me out?

By the time she reaches the office doorway, Kaia's palms are damp with nervous sweat. Hunter doesn't hesitate before sweeping into the dimly lit space, immediately planting herself in the furthest of two chairs and squaring her shoulders like she's steeling herself for battle. Kaia draws her brows together, confused at the display. It seems like whatever this meeting is about, it wasn't the lieutenant's idea. Resisting the urge to linger in the doorway a few seconds too long, Kaia scrambles to paste on an equally stony expression before venturing into whatever hidden threat awaits her.

"Have a seat, Montgomery," the captain rumbles without even glancing up from his computer screen. "We need to discuss some... concerns that have been brought to my attention."

The ominous statement hangs in the stale office air as Kaia trades a loaded look with her lieutenant. Hunter's jaw is set in a mulish line that suggests she's likely biting back a stream of insubordinate questions, as if she might demand at any moment that the captain just spit out whatever it is he's taking his sweet time to say.

Why does she look so tense?

Amidst her confusion, Kaia can't help but admire her superior's piercing blue eyes that seem to glint with a permanent inferno of defiant spirit. She muses that they are not too different, Hunter and herself. The thought makes the corner of her mouth twitch with a threatening smile, and Hunter's brows draw together in an expression torn between outrage and curiosity. Clearly, she'd be interested to know what could possibly have Kaia smirking in such a situation as this. Their silent standoff is broken as the captain finally raises his head.

"Several of the other recruits have expressed doubts about Montgomery's ability to keep up during training exercises," he states without preamble, making Kaia instantly bristle. "Questioning whether her...dedication to the program will hold up under the pressures of actual field scenarios."

The words hang there like a challenge as the captain watches for Kaia's reaction. Her vision practically turns red with humiliation and disgust that those sneering frat clowns had tried to sabotage her already, barely a week into training. She opens her mouth to launch a furious defense, but Hunter beats her to the punch.

"With all due respect, Sir, that's a load of bull—"

"Lieutenant," Hewitt cuts her off with a raised palm and a warning glare, his tone brokering no argument yet. "I'm not accusing anyone of anything. You know I value your leadership more than anyone's in this district, and I've heard your praise for Montgomery's abilities."

Kaia tries not to preen at the revelation that the fearsome lieutenant had been discussing her, praising her.

"But we clearly have a division problem in our ranks, and that doesn't bode well for effective rescue services."

Hunter's jaw works stubbornly for a moment before she gives a terse nod, clearly swallowing the slew of angry retorts she'd been prepared to unleash. But Kaia's outrage is still bubbling in the back of her throat. Who the hell do those pampered frat bros think they are? Undermining her right out of the gate because their fragile little egos can't handle a woman working harder than them? Just the thought of their sneering conde-scension makes her blood boil, fists clenching against her thighs.

"I know that proving yourselves as capable is probably at the forefront of both of your minds every day in this job. And that none of the rest of us will ever quite understand what that's like. However," the captain continues in that low grumble, "you have to admit, Hunter, Montgomery has a certain... reputation around here already. For being a little too eager to jump into the fray without coordinating first."

"Honing a recruit's eagerness into streamlined efficiency is part of the job, Sir. My training program has barely begun," Hunter instantly fires back. "Montgomery's drive and capabilities are a credit to this station. If her teammates can't appreciate having such a fearless addition to their ranks, that's a poor reflection on their own commitment, not hers."

Kaia somehow manages to keep her expression somewhat neutral as the captain and the lieutenant continue their terse back and forth. But inside, a raging battle of emotions is threatening to force up her lunch. The fury at her crewmates is still rearing its ugly head, but now it's competing for space against a swelling pride and a glimmer of hope in her gut. Watching Hunter defend her so fiercely is clouding Kaia's vision with a rose-colored tint.

The captain is suggesting something about extra one-on-one training sessions with Hunter to "offer extra guidance on effectively working alongside the male rookies." But his gravelly words are just noise droning in Kaia's ears as flashes of memories bombard her from working alongside those overgrown toddlers.

Cochran's ugly sneer as she blew past him on their last sprint circuit... The muttered slurs when she stuck that perfect reverse landing from the forty-foot tower... Every dismissive scoff and sidelong glare like they couldn't believe a woman would dare walk onto their playing field.

Kaia grits her teeth, battling to keep her fury in check as Hunter nods reluctantly at whatever extra training regimen the captain has proposed. They both flick assessing glances Kaia's way every so often, as if waiting for her to arrogantly fly off the handle.

Well, they can both keep waiting. I won't give those pathetic brats out there the satisfaction.

Catching the slightest hint of sympathy in both of their gazes is enough to solidify her resolve. She refuses to be pitied, especially by Hunter. The one person in this station who she desperately wants to respect her. To even see her as an equal one day, maybe. This brilliant, fearless woman has spent her whole careering facing down the same brand of toxic misogyny that is swarming around Kaia right now, and she's still standing. A glorious example of pure tenacity. Just watching her chest rise and fall with each controlled inhale makes Kaia's heart swell with admiration. This shit won't happen when Hunter someday sits on the other side of that desk.

The captain's brusque dismissal finally cuts through the whirlwind of Kaia's emotions. She pushes to her feet, shoulders squared, and stalks from his office without a word. Feeling the weight of Hunter's searching stare as she goes, Kaia doesn't don't dare turn back and let her see the simmering fury in her eyes. Or the steadily growing attraction.

White knuckling the steering wheel for the entire drive home, Kaia barely makes it to the privacy of her own apartment before the dam breaks. After slamming the door behind her, she rips off her sweat-stained undershirt and uniform pants. Flinging them violently across the cramped living room, her rage finally boils over.

"How *dare* they!" she shrieks, raking her hands over her head. Her tightly curled hair tendrils are bursting from the rigid confines of her carefully twisted bun, left, right, and center. The shock and outrage that had flooded her at the station churns and remolds itself into staggering disbelief. Sure, she knew they sneered at her, looked down on her. But to sink so low as to badmouth her to the captain? To whisper poison in his ear that she's too weak for the job?

Kaia never saw it coming. She had thought high school ended years ago, for all of them.

She paces the confines of the tiny square space like a caged lioness, gripped by the overwhelming urge to hit something, break something, unleash this torrent of frustration somehow. All the while, her dad's voice is echoing in her skull.

"Who would ever take a female firefighter seriously? Stay in your own lane, Kaia. Leave the tough jobs to the men... You have a real pretty face, kiddo. You ever considered teaching kindergarten?"

Her breaths come in short, harsh pants, blood boiling hotter as visions of her dad's patronizing smile melt and blur, replaced by flickers of dismissive sneers and muttered slurs from her crewmates. The growing crowd of naysayers presses in on her like the looming, white walls. Suffocating the inferno of her fury until it starts to bank.

What if I can't endure this fight for the rest of my damn career?

The vicious, unbidden thought pierces straight through the swirling red of her fury like a frozen dagger. She halts mid-pace, swaying a little as a wrecking ball of doubt crashes through her ribcage. Kaia has never doubted her own capabilities, her enduring strength, but she had also never stopped to think for a minute about the steady, eroding exhaustion she'd have to bear battling everyone else's doubts day after day.

The fight drains out of her in a rush, leaving her hollowed out and tired in her very bones. She crumples sideways onto the couch, burying her face in trembling hands as the waves of uncertainty threaten to drown her.

But then, another face swims into her mind.

The memory of Lieutenant Hunter's fiery defense in the captain's office, the blaze of pride flickering in those bright, blue eyes as she stood up for Kaia's honor.

She believes in Kaia, in her right to a position on her crew.

Wiping her eyes, Kaia pushes up from the sagging couch cushions with renewed determination. If Hunter believed she could carry on the fight and win, she sure as hell wasn't going to let her down.

Kaia makes the silent vow to herself, and to Hunter, and to every other woman in their field who has to tirelessly rage against being dismissed by arrogant neanderthals. As her resolve is forged iron-clad in her veins, a glorious desert sunset slants through her window. The fiery orange glow like a sign, illuminating her path forward.

5

HALLIE

The slight chill of the early morning desert air nips at Hallie's exposed skin as she hops out of her truck in the almost empty parking lot of Fire Station 3. She shrugs her jacket tighter around her shoulders, partly to ward off the cold, but mostly to disguise the tremble in her hands. Her pulse has been thrumming with a restless energy ever since she opened her eyes a full hour before her alarm this morning.

She had to begrudgingly admit, these one-to-one training sessions with Montgomery were a decent idea from the captain. The showboating has to stop, and Kaia needs to learn communication and protocol in an environment where she isn't constantly tempted to lash out at her crew-mates. Hallie understood better than anyone the urge to reject the rest of the recruits before they had a chance to demonstrate how thoroughly they would reject her. But the division in the squad will get someone hurt sooner or later. Montgomery needs to learn to fall in line, while not also feeling like she's been bullied into submission.

Glaring as they are, however, none of these truths were what had Hallie's skin prickling with anticipation in the time it took her to roll out of bed and make her way here at the crack of dawn. Fact is, Hallie is stupidly looking forward to the chance to be alone with Montgomery. Ever since the captain suggested the private sessions, she's been haunted by images of that powerful frame glistening with sweat, of her dark eyes flaring with determination as she pushes to impress her lieutenant. Hallie had tried to ignore it in regular training, but she couldn't help feeling more and more like Montgomery's performances were intended to impress *her* more than the other rookies.

Get a grip, Hallie.

This undeniable attraction between them is fast becoming a dangerous distraction. A fresh wave of anxiety mingles with the anticipation writhing in Hallie's gut as she makes her way towards the station building. She wants more than anything to explore this connection she feels, and she's sure that Montgomery feels the same way—at least, if her little demonstration in the showers is anything to go by—but Hallie can't shake the fear that anything happening between them would damage both of their careers. Shaking her head against her warring thoughts, she pushes through the heavy door into the training facility, steeling herself for a totally professional training session.

Of course, Montgomery isn't going to make it easy.

Feet planted at either side of a stretching mat, Kaia is bent at the waist, her sinfully peachy ass thrust straight in the air.

Lord, help me.

Hallie forces herself not to stare as she marches across the garage, sheepishly glancing side to side to check no other colleagues are present to enjoy the show.

"Good morning, Lieutenant." Montgomery's greeting is a low rumble, muffled slightly as she presses her fingertips into the mat. The coy rasp in her tone has Hallie's mouth instantly going dry.

"Montgomery," she grits out, sounding harsher

than she had intended. She quickly tears her gaze away from the hypnotic stretch of Montgomery's form-fitting workout attire, hugging every delicious curve. "I trust you're ready for a focused training session this morning?"

"Oh, I'm ready," Kaia practically purrs, before she languidly unfurls to her full height. She twists at the waist, those intense brown eyes immediately seeking Hallie's as she raises one sculpted arm in an overhead stretch. It's only too tempting for Hallie to be enraptured by the rippling contours of her bicep, the tantalizing sliver of revealed midriff as her shirt rides up over those chiseled abs. The lieutenant gives herself a harsh inward shake, heat flooding her cheeks. With an impassive clearing of her throat, she nods toward the staging area.

"Let's get to it then. We'll start with sprints and communication relays. You're falling way behind on grasping those particular skills."

A spark flashes in Montgomery's eyes and Hallie knows her criticism has struck a nerve. The obstinate rookie lifts her chin in blatant challenge, a rakish smirk slowly blooming over her full, tempting lips.

"Whatever you say, Lieutenant," she tosses over her shoulder, already striding away. Her hips sway with that same arrogant swagger that drives Hallie crazy. "Just try to keep up."

The next forty-five minutes is a blistering gauntlet of start-stop sprints while Hallie and Montgomery bellow coded instructions back and forth. The commanding officer keeps her tone as clipped and authoritative as she can muster, attempting to squash any hint of the lingering want simmering in her veins. It proves nearly impossible, what with the rich rasp of Kaia's sexy laughter floating across the mats between repetitions. Hallie finds her mind wandering, clouded with daydreams of Montgomery's breath washing over her face, her lips tantalizingly close. Close enough for Hallie to lean in and capture them with her own...

"Lieutenant! Did you get that?"

Kaia's bemused demand cuts straight through her lieutenant's distracted fantasies like a bucket of ice water. Hallie's heart jackhammers in stunned panic as she realizes she's been too preoccupied to even register the rookie's last slew of code-shouting. Of course, the sniggering Montgomery called her on it, that cocky shit is never one to let an opportunity at showing off go to waste.

"Give it a rest, Montgomery!" Hallie instantly

snaps, prowling closer to where Kaia stands, doubled over with her hands braced on her knees. The heave of her breasts is far too alluring this close up. "We're supposed to be improving your team communication, not fueling your idiotic need to one-up your superiors!"

Kaia's laughter rings out again, though this time the teasing cadence is laced with a touch of exertion. Before she can help herself, Hallie's mind runs away from her again, flooded with the desire to lick the sweat from the hollow of Montgomery's throat.

"C'mon, Lieutenant. Am I really such a nuisance?" That wicked mouth stretches into a wolfish grin as she shifts her stance, openly allowing her gaze to roam brazenly over Hallie's sweat-slick tank top. "Guess I'm not trying hard enough to impress you."

There's a deliberate, unabashed invitation in her purring tone. She prowls a little closer as if she's just waiting for Hallie to cave and crush their bodies together, catching those plump lips in a searing kiss. At hearing Montgomery confirm her efforts to impress her, Hallie's breath catches, the electric current sparking between them dialing up a few thousand volts. All she would have to do is close the final scant inches between their heaving chests.

And kiss my shot at captain goodbye.

"Enough of that," the lieutenant bites out, teeth gritted more against her own burning desire than Montgomery's blatant flirting. "You're here to save lives, not to earn a gold star from teacher. Go and grab some water before I have you sprinting until your legs give out."

Montgomery's only response is a dark, knowing chuckle as she obediently turns towards the break room. Hallie clenches her jaw, trying not to watch the delicious roll of her hips in those skintight yoga pants. As soon as the door from the training area swings shut, she bolts for the locker room to splash cold water over her scorching skin. Silently berating herself in the mirror, Hallie quickly realizes these private training sessions are going to be a twisted kind of torture. She's not sure what she did to deserve such bittersweet suffering. And she knows it's not going to get any easier.

When the lieutenant returns to the training area, suitably cooled off, she finds Kaia back on her stretching mat. There's a feisty challenge glinting in her dark eyes. She arches a brow, silently daring Hallie to try and break that cocky spirit.

Instead of bristling against the rookie's blatant arrogance, Hallie finds herself softening in the face of such raw determination. That intense desire to constantly prove herself, to never show weakness or fatigue, the lieutenant recognizes that desperate drive all too well. A sad, nostalgic smile tugs at her own lips as she takes a seat on the mat across from Kaia's relaxed form.

"Not going to lie, Montgomery," she begins, rolling her tight shoulders to release some of the lingering tension coiled there. "Watching you show up every day prepared to put on a one-man circus reminds me of my own rookie days with the brigade."

Kaia's brows quirk, no doubt surprised by the conversational shift in Hallie's demeanor. She wraps her arms around her knees, curiosity kindling behind her calmer expression.

"Shocking as it may seem, I wasn't always so effortlessly superior to my crewmates," Hallie continues, the playful barb drawing a low, rasping chuckle from between Kaia's glistening lips.

For a long moment Hallie only watches her chest rise and fall, mesmerized by the tantalizing slide of perspiration over her sculpted collarbones. She has to force herself to meet Kaia's molten gaze. "Truth is, I come from a long line of fire chiefs and strong leaders. Busting my ass to prove I was tough enough to fill their damn boots was the only thing that mattered back then."

The warmth in Kaia's expression shifts into something deeper, more pensive. A shared understanding of their endless battle to be respected as equals in an oppressively masculine world.

"My old man thought thirty years on the police force made him an expert on what women are and aren't capable of." The rigidity of Kaia's jawline makes Hallie think her upbringing wasn't quite so supportive as the home of the Hunters.

"If he'd had his way, I'd probably be teaching finger painting classes instead of fighting to prove my strength alongside the men every day. He was so pissed when I turned down a free ride to nursing school that we didn't talk for over a year."

A sad smile twists Hallie's lips in response.

"I can't imagine what that must have been like. Pop was thrilled when I said I wanted to follow in his footsteps. My fear of never living up to his name formed in my own head, long before any rookie asshole taunted me with it out loud."

"But you still took that risk," Kaia rasps, the barest hint of awe lacing her tone. It warms Hallie in a way no amount of desert sun ever could. "You proved you were worthy of the legacy over and over until they couldn't ignore or dismiss you anymore."

The naked admiration in her soft utterance is nothing short of electrifying. They hold each other's stare for a suspended moment, the pulsing silence seeming to shrink the world down to this tiny sanctuary between them.

"You'll get there too, Montgomery. The rest of those sorry recruits might hate you for wiping the floor with them every day, but they'll learn to respect you for it."

She huffs a small laugh. "Would it be wildly against protocol if you called me Kaia?"

Hallie's heart thunders with a wild yearning to reach out and brush her knuckles over the sharp angle of Kaia's cheekbone, let her palm cup the strength pulsing in the hollow of her throat.

Ever the bolder of the two of them, Kaia leans forward, their tense breath mingling as their eyes remain locked on each other. All concerns about her position fly from Hallie's mind as she inches closer to the glistening temptation of Kaia's lips.

"Only as inappropriate as it would be for you to start calling me Hallie," she murmurs, brushing the tip of Kaia's sweat-slicked nose with her own.

Then the metallic clang of the main doors being thrown open slams through the fragile stillness like a bucket of ice water. Kaia and Hallie spring apart, whipping their heads around as shuffling footsteps and raucous chatter echoes from the corridor. The rest of the rookie class is marching in for morning formation.

Hallie's gaze flies back to Kaia just as she jolts upright to her full height, self-consciously raking her fingers through her wild, mussed dark curls. The look of confusion and frustration mirrored on her face is nearly enough to obliterate every ounce of professional distance Hallie has been clinging to.

She wants to grab Kaia by those bulging biceps and crush their bodies together. Finally give in to the gnawing ache that's been building between them all morning and lose herself completely in her intoxicating heat.

But it's already too late. The first wave of rowdy recruits comes tumbling into the training area, jostling between themselves like a pack of overgrown, overconfident pups. Mercifully, none of them seem to register the yearning tension still thrumming between the lieutenant and her favorite student. Even so, the intimate moment is well and truly shattered.

Rising to her feet, Hallie composes her features into an impassive mask and ushers Kaia toward the crowd with a subtle dip of her chin.

She can't bring herself to meet her eyes, unsure whether she'll find relief or devastation reflected there.

This maddening attraction is quickly spiraling out of her control.

As much as she tries to douse the flames with all the self-control she can muster, Hallie has a sinking feeling she's in grave danger of getting burned.

6

KAIA

Kaia's heart is still thundering as she strides to join her crewmates for roll call, the ghost of Hallie's breath still lingering on her lips. She fights to school her guilty expression, to stamp down the raging want still coiling low in her belly from their heated almost-kiss.

Hallie had been so tantalizingly close, close enough for Kaia to drown in the azure pools of her eyes, to trace the sharp lines of her jaw with her fingertips. She had been powerless to resist, throwing caution to the wind as she had leaned in to obliterate the charged boundary between her and her superior. And for one delirious, endless moment it had seemed like Hallie might finally give in.

But of course, the arrival of the other rookies had shattered that fragile tension just when things were about to combust between them. Hallie had coolly reassembled her professional mask as always, not even daring to meet Kaia's eyes as she ushered her toward their crewmates. Leaving Kaia to wonder, not for the first time, if this crackling heat between them was recklessly one-sided after all.

Maybe she had only imagined the reciprocal want darkening Hallie's eyes to swirling storms. The same blazing desire Kaia felt every time she drank in the lieutenant's powerful presence. Every passing minute of their private training sessions had slowly been driving Kaia to unravel at the seams.

Well, she supposes as she takes her position alongside the other rookies for inspection, *at least the bitter sting of rejection won't be anything new.*

Straightening her shoulders, Kaia clears her hazy thoughts and concentrates on the morning briefing. Her pulse still hammers with chaotic adrenaline, but she forces herself to keep her expression as coolly impassive as Hallie's always is.

As though absolutely nothing had occurred between them mere minutes ago.

Of course, controlling her restless desire for the lieutenant proves to be the least of her worries, as the sudden blaring signal of an emergency call-out rings throughout the station.

Hallie immediately assumes command, calling out the report of a raging house fire in a residential neighborhood nearby. She barks precise instructions, and Kaia springs into action with her fellow rookies.

The metallic wail of the truck sirens proves effective in yanking Kaia fully back into the moment with harsh clarity.

This was real, this was what she had been training so relentlessly for all along.

No more time to dwell on the heated morning with her fiery commander, they had a job: save lives at any cost.

The smoke is already thick and acrid when they arrive on the scene, the house nearly engulfed in blinding shades of orange and red. Lieutenant Hunter's authoritative bark rings out over the chaos as the engine roars to a halt, throwing the crew into a seamless flurry of coordinated response. Within seconds, Kaia has her mask secure, helmet on and a hose in hand, eyes flicking back and forth between her crewmates and their leader.

I won't let her down today.

Though she knows better than to be distracted on the job, Kaia can't help the possessive rush that comes over her at drinking in the sight of Hallie at her peak—jaw taut with intense focus, every muscle toned and primed as she deftly maneuvers her team into position. Kaia's admiration only burns more feverishly at the unwavering confidence with which Hallie commands her role in the field. Her lieutenant is poetry in motion, magnetic and unstoppable.

Squashing down the forbidden embers of attraction, Kaia hurls herself fully into attacking the blaze with the rest of her crewmates. Sweat instantly soaks her uniform as scorching smoke plumes around her, the roaring hiss of the pressurized hoses filling the air with their deafening white noise.

For several endless minutes, Kaia loses herself completely in the adrenaline-spiked focus of combating the relentless torrent of flame and fumes. She works flawlessly alongside her unit, seamlessly alternating positions and hose trajectories without having to so much as raise their voices over the din. A savage thrill surges through her at how synchronized they've become, the culmination of Hallie's grueling training finally paying off in the field.

They have the makings of a proper crew, moving and breathing as one.

Just as that rush of hard-earned pride swells in Kaia's chest, a noise abruptly cuts through the chaos. She snaps her head up in alarm. Over the shriek of the water cannons and the roar of the devouring blaze, she's certain she can hear a faint, pitiful whining of an animal's muffled cries.

Without a second thought for protocol, she slams her end of the hose into Cochran's hands with a terse shout to take over. He gapes at her in bewilderment as she sprints away, barreling towards the smoke, her senses straining to pinpoint where the noise is coming from.

The heat sears her skin even through her protective gear as she surges through the house. She hears Cochran's alarmed shout behind her but presses on, laser-focused on locating the source of those cries.

There!

Toward the very back of the building, a

mournful bark echoes. Kaia can't see anything through the smoke but she follows the sound to what she is pretty sure is the kitchen.

Without pausing to consider the risk, Kaia begins to clamber over the fallen debris in her path, swerving and bending to avoid the remnants of blackened beams sagging from the ceiling.

The seconds seem to blur into one dizzying, scorching haze as she ventures through the heart of the rapidly consuming inferno. Her pulse roaring in her ears is almost loud enough to drown out the bone-shaking screech of the crumbling structure.

Finally making it across the charred rubble, she stoops to grab the trapped dog in a blind rush, hissing when a shard of wood stabs at her gloved palm.

"Easy there, buddy," she murmurs as she slips her own mask free and holds it over the dog's muzzle giving him air. "I've got you now, you're gonna be just fine."

With a gentleness that seems at odds with the sheer power of her frame, Kaia carefully scoops the quaking pet into her arms, keeping him swathed in the folds of her coat. She has to get them out of here fast before the flaming debris raining down around them blocks their path.

A deafening crack explodes over her head, and she instinctively curls herself over the dog's trembling form as a jagged chunk of plaster crashes onto the space she had occupied only moments ago.

Chest heaving against the toxic smoke, Kaia shoves off at a desperate sprint, following the path back out she had forged on her way in.

Every bone in her body screams in protest against the blistering heat, but the precious cargo whimpering in her arms keeps her bolting forward with her remaining strength.

At last, Kaia bursts back into the smoke-hazed daylight, gulping down cleaner air in deep, convulsive gasps. But no sooner does she stumble from the red-hazed danger zone than a furious shout rings out and a blurred figure storms towards her.

Hallie's electric eyes seem to bore directly through Kaia's very soul. Without another word she knows that the look on her lieutenant's face doesn't bode well at all.

Kaia barely has time to carefully hand the wounded pup to a paramedic before Hallie is on her, grabbing her roughly by the bicep and dragging her to the relative safety of the sidewalk.

"What the hell were you thinking, Montgomery?!" The lieutenant's shout makes Kaia wince, while the tumultuous mix of fury and terror plastered on Hallie's face takes her aback. "You never, NEVER enter a burning building without backup and a goddamn *plan*! We never go alone!! You could have been killed in there!"

Despite the blistering heat still pulsing from the flames at her back, Kaia feels an icy chill lance through her at the raw anguish contorting Hallie's beautiful features. She opens her mouth to defend herself, to insist that she had no choice but to save the helpless animal. But Hallie's hands tighten on her shoulders, giving her a rough shake that rattles Kaia to her core.

"I don't want to hear it! You completely flouted protocol and put your own life at risk!" Hallie's chest heaves with the force of her tirade. "Get your ass back on the truck. Now!"

With that, the lieutenant releases her grip and storms away, barking orders at the rest of the crew still working to fully contain the blaze. Kaia stands rooted to the spot for a long moment, her heart jackhammering against her ribs as she watches Hallie's retreating form.

Swallowing hard against the acrid taste of smoke and shame, Kaia slowly makes her way back to the engine, every muscle aching with fatigue and the aftershocks of adrenaline. She passes the rest of the crew without a word, jaw clenched as she stares straight ahead, not daring to meet their no doubt smug stares.

The ride back to the station is thick with silent tension, broken only by the occasional crackle of the radio. Kaia can feel Hallie's molten glare boring into the side of her head from the seat next to her but refuses to acknowledge it, her pride still smarting from being dressed down like an errant child in front of the rest of the crew.

It's not until they've arrived back at the station and the rest of the guys have filed out of the vehicle that Hallie finally breaks the suffocating silence between them.

"Locker room. Now," she grits out, not even sparing Kaia a glance as she jumps down from the cab and slams the door with enough force to rattle Kaia's teeth.

Heart in her throat, Kaia follows after her,

steeling herself for the impending confrontation. She finds Hallie pacing like a caged tiger in front of the lockers, hands clenching and unclenching at her sides. As soon as Kaia shuts the door to their female-only safe zone, Hallie rounds on her, eyes flashing.

"Do you have any idea how stupid that little stunt was? What were you trying to prove back there?"

Kaia bristles at the scathing accusation in Hallie's tone, her own temper flaring to life. "I was trying to save a life! Isn't that what we're supposed to do?"

"Not at the expense of your own!" Hallie takes a menacing step forward, crowding into Kaia's space until they're practically nose to nose. The charged energy crackling between them is so intense Kaia swears she can taste it on her tongue.

"You are not invincible, Montgomery. I don't care how badly you want to be the hero. You follow protocol or you'll get yourself killed!"

"Why do you even care so much? It's my life to risk!" The words explode from Kaia's lips before she can stop them, her fists clenched at her sides to keep from reaching up and clasping Hallie's face.

For a moment, Hallie looks as if Kaia had struck her. Something agonized and raw flashes across her face, there and gone again in an instant. When she speaks again, her voice is deadly soft.

"You're under my command. Your safety is my responsibility. And I'll be damned if I let you throw your life away on my watch just to prove you have balls."

They stare at each other for a seemingly endless moment, chests heaving and pulses roaring in the suffocating silence between them.

This time, there's no one to interrupt them as Kaia fists the front of Hallie's shirt and hauls her against her body. Their lips collide in a frenzied kiss, Hallie crowding Kaia back into the wall of lockers behind her.

Greedily exploring Hallie's body with slightly trembling hands, Kaia reaches the lieutenant's waist and immediately yanks her shirt free from the confines of her belt. She releases a satisfied groan as her fingers make contact with Hallie's sweat-slicked skin, consumed by the thrill of finally crashing through the barrier that had held them both back.

"Whatever you're thinking, we don't have time," Hallie whispers through a breathless chuckle. "The guys will be showered and gathered for the debriefing soon."

"Well then, Lieutenant, you had better debrief *me* pretty quick, don't you think?"

Hallie's answering laugh is louder this time, she nips playfully at Kaia's lips before plunging her tongue back into her mouth. The heavy exhaustion from this morning's rescue has dissipated completely and Kaia's blood is singing with wanton desire. She grips the firm cheeks of Hallie's ass and grinds her hips into her own, desperate for her body to be as close as humanly possible.

Kaia barely represses an outraged whine when Hallie eventually breaks their kiss, panting slightly as she backs away. But the devious smirk spreading across her lieutenant's face tells her this is not quite over.

"We better hit the showers, Montgomery. You taste like charcoal."

Kaia huffs an amused snort as she makes a show of sniffing her armpit, before promptly tearing her shirt over her head. She relishes in the way Hallie's eyes rove shamelessly over her body, while she quickly shrugs out of her own uniform.

They are both a mess of stumbling limbs, shucking off their boots and discarding their underwear in a haphazard trail towards the showers.

Thank fuck we have this locker room all to ourselves.

Kaia gasps at the shock of cold water that hits her shoulders when Hallie shoves her back into a cubicle, but the stream soon heats up, trickling over their sticky skin. Spurned on by the fact they only have a few minutes before their absence becomes suspicious, Kaia immediately dips her head and draws Hallie's nipple into her mouth. She wants to claim as much of her skin as she can before they're forced to dry off and slip back into work mode.

Hallie's head drops back as she moans, fisting the back of Kaia's unruly curls while she nips and sucks at each breast in turn. The rush in Kaia's veins is overwhelming. She devours her lieutenant's body like a starving animal, reveling in the deep groans that rumble through Hallie's chest. She releases her own soft yelp when Hallie pulls her head up by the scalp and presses her back against the wall with a consuming kiss.

Whatever lines they're crossing, whatever risks they might be taking with their own careers, they're the last thing on Kaia's mind as she tastes nothing but restless lust on her lieutenant's tongue.

7

HALLIE

Simmering with impatient desire, Hallie trails her hands lower, grazing Kaia's hips with her blunt nails. Anxiety dances at the back of her mind, the reminder that they can't linger here too long. But the temptation of Kaia's naked body is too much to bear, and Hallie's attention is quickly consumed with chasing the rivulets of water down Kaia's abs with her tongue.

Dropping to her knees, Hallie locks eyes with the panting rookie. She can't help but smirk as Kaia's gaze widens in surprise.

"You better clean that grime off your skin sharpish, rookie. I've got things covered down here."

Kaia's head drops back against the wall as

Hallie hoists her leg over her shoulder and sucks a line of bruising kisses from her knee to the apex of her spread thighs. Then, running her nose through the thick curls gathered there, the lieutenant glances up again.

"Am I distracting you, Kaia? Soap. Now."

The rookie huffs out a small giggle and grabs the shower gel from the shelf beside her. She squirts it into her hand, but promptly has to shove her face into the crook of her elbow to muffle a strangled moan. Hallie has clamped her lips around her swollen clit. Almost rolling her eyes back at the musky taste, the lieutenant laps and sucks at Kaia's slick pussy, wishing she had the time to really draw this out.

As it is, she has to get this done fast.

She doesn't want to leave this cubicle until Kaia has come apart right on her face.

Spreading Kaia more with her other hand, Hallie plunges two fingers inside her, pumping a few times before adding another and curling them both towards her palm. Kaia is wet and ready. Kaia's breaths are coming short and sharp now, her hips grinding against Hallie's greedy mouth as she starts to fuck herself on Hallie's fingers.

When Kaia's legs begin to shake, the lieutenant

is certain she's getting close. Hallie dives back in to suck her clit into her mouth, all the while thrusting her fingers in and out in a punishing rhythm.

In just seconds, Hallie feels Kaia clenching and pulsing around her hand. The lieutenant grunts as the rookie's weight presses down on her shoulder. She is clearly struggling to stand through the onslaught of her sudden climax. Hallie's cheeks begin to ache with a satisfied grin as she continues to lap and kiss until she feels the aftershocks begin to fade.

Rising to her feet, Hallie reaches for the soap for herself, relishing Kaia's blissed out expression. She leans in to plant a tender kiss on the rookie's lips.

Two. Three.

The two of them share a breathless chuckle as they lean their foreheads against each other. But when Kaia moves to reach between Hallie's legs, she grabs her by the wrist and shakes her head.

"Go get dried off, Montgomery. You better be at debriefing before your scary lieutenant arrives."

"Hunter, a moment please."

Captain Hewitt's gruff summons stops Hallie in her tracks as she strides past his office, having just dismissed her crew from the house-fire debriefing.

Unease pools thickly in her stomach.

She steps into the captain's dimly lit office, the heavy oak door clicking shut behind her. She can't shake the ominous certainty that this conversation will center around a certain headstrong recruit.

"Sir," she greets with a respectful nod, lowering herself into the chair across from his, knuckles white where they grip its polished wooden arms. "What can I do for you?"

Hewitt steeples his fingers beneath his chin, his piercing gaze pinning Hallie like a hapless butterfly to a board. She fights the urge to squirm under that penetrating assessment, forcibly calming her breathing as she braces for his response.

"Just checking in on the progress of the rookie class in light of the call out today," the captain begins, his tone carefully neutral. "Your initial estimation of their capabilities, problem areas that need addressing. The usual."

Hallie gives a stiff nod, her jaw working as she chews over her response. She knows she needs to tread cautiously here, avoid drawing undue attention to any single recruit. Especially one whose mere presence seems to light Hallie's blood on fire these days.

The lieutenant clears her throat and blinks rapidly as images of Kaia's naked, dripping curves merrily flit behind her eyelids.

She can still taste Kaia's orgasm on her tongue and she likes it.

"Overall, they're shaping up to be a solid crew," she says, hoping her voice reflects only cool professionalism. "A few attitude adjustments needed here and there, but nothing that can't be corrected with more time and experience in the field."

Hewitt hums, his expression inscrutable as he leans back in his chair, fingers drumming an idle rhythm against the desktop.

"Attitude adjustments," he muses, bushy brows drawing together. "That's a rather diplomatic way of putting it."

Hallie feels her cheeks flush hotly at the captain's pointed observation, cursing herself for reacting to his obvious bait.

"Sir, I can assure you, Montgomery's...willful methods are being addressed in our private training."

"Ah yes, about that." Hewitt's lips thin into a grim line, his tone sharpening. "Tell me, Hunter, how is that going? Because from where I'm sitting, it looks like your recruit is still prone to acting on dangerous impulse with zero regard for the safety of herself or her team."

A lance of possessive fury pierces through Hallie's chest at the captain's blunt accusation, the knee-jerk instinct to defend Kaia's character rearing its stubborn head.

"With respect, Captain," Hallie grits out, "Montgomery's actions, while ill-advised, directly saved the life of a trapped civilian. Her quick thinking and fearless initiative are assets to this department, not liabilities."

Hewitt's steely eyes narrow, his chin jutting forward in unmistakable challenge.

"That defense reeks of bullshit, Lieutenant. What's going on with you? Are you really prepared to stake your reputation on the actions of a green recruit you've known for less than a month?"

Hallie opens her mouth to argue, to insist on Kaia's potential, but Hewitt cuts her off with a sharp raise of his hand.

"I'm not finished. Your job as commanding officer is to assess and lead this rookie class with complete objectivity. To make the hard calls regarding their abilities and adherence to protocol, without allowing personal feelings to cloud your judgment."

The captain's voice gentles slightly, taking on an almost fatherly edge that raises the fine hairs at Hallie's nape.

"I understand you want to champion Montgomery as a fellow woman. Hell, I want to see her succeed just as badly, if she's truly got the goods. But you cannot appear to play favorites here, Hunter. Not when your position in this department is at stake."

Hewitt leans forward again, his gaze boring into Hallie's with unnerving intensity.

"If you keep leaping to defend a single recruit's poor choices at the expense of the group, you risk losing the respect of the very men and women you've fought to lead. Is coddling Montgomery really worth throwing all that away?"

Silence stretches between them, heavy with the weight of Hewitt's warning. Hallie can feel the blood drain from her face as the gravity of the situation sinks in, chilling her to the bone. Because as much as she wants to keep arguing on Kaia's behalf, a small, traitorously rational voice whispers that the captain is right. Hallie's feelings for Kaia, as fierce and intoxicating as they are, are clouding her objectivity. Influencing her to make allowances that she wouldn't dream of extending to any other rookie under her command.

Shame burns like acrid bile in the back of Hallie's throat as she averts her eyes, unable to hold Hewitt's probing stare a second longer.

"You're right, sir," she responds, the admission tasting like bitter ashes on her tongue. "It won't happen again. I'll be...stricter with Montgomery going forward. Rein in the reckless behavior."

"Good." Hewitt settles back in his chair, looking appeased. "You're one of the best lieutenants I've ever seen, Hunter. I'd hate to see you throw away such a promising future over a rookie who still has a hell of a lot to learn about being a team player."

Hallie can only nod, her heart twisting painfully in her chest. Continuing to play the hard-ass, uncompromising lieutenant is the last thing she wants to do now when it comes to Kaia. Not with the terrifying emotion that's burrowing its way into her chest. Lingering on her skin.

But it's clear that she doesn't have a choice. Not

if she wants to protect both their careers and maintain the integrity of her team.

Hewitt clears his throat, drawing Hallie from her sullen spiral with a start.

"That'll be all, Lieutenant. Keep me updated on the progress of the rookie evaluations. Especially any...problem areas that need further addressing."

The clear dismissal rings with unspoken warning, a reminder of the scrutiny Hallie and Kaia will now be under. Hallie rises on leaden legs, throwing a mock salute before making her escape. She marches down the hallway in a daze, her head swimming as she tries to process the rollercoaster of a day.

As much as she wants to keep denying it, to cling to the feverish belief that this infatuation with Kaia is harmless, she knows deep in her bones that it's a lit fuse poised to blow.

And when it does, the collateral damage won't be limited to singed fingers and wounded pride. It will be the total destruction of everything Hallie has sacrificed and strived for. The inevitable implosion of her own career and Kaia's right along with it.

The certainty of that danger galvanizes Hallie's

resolve as she reaches the locker room, grateful to find it empty. She sinks onto a bench, dropping her face into trembling hands.

She has to end this dance with Kaia before it's too late. Before her growing attachment compromises her ability to be the firm lieutenant. How could she train Kaia's brazen attitude into strict obedience when it's the very thing that draws her in?

But *damn* if the mere thought of pushing Kaia away, of watching the hope gutter and die in those molten eyes, doesn't flay Hallie raw. Peel back the layers of staunch discipline and self-control to expose the ravenous ache beneath. The intense yearning for even a fleeting taste of the inferno raging between them, consequences be damned.

She huffs out an exasperated groan, scrubbing at her eyes.

How the hell am I gonna deal with this?

8

KAIA

The next morning's training passes by in a tense blur.

A churning anxiety takes root in the pit of Kaia's stomach when Hallie spends the entirety of their private session maintaining a firm distance, offering only clipped instructions and short breaks between exercises that barely give Kaia time to breathe.

Let alone question the lieutenant's cold attitude.

By the time the other rookies show up for the start of regular training, Kaia is utterly convinced that Hallie is pushing her away on purpose. The weight of the rejection is more crushing than Kaia could have ever anticipated, having replayed the memory of their hurried intimacy in the showers countless times the prior evening.

She couldn't understand it. Hallie had seemed just as desperate for it as Kaia had been.

Why is she trying to act like nothing happened?

Kaia's heart races as she spots Hallie hunched over a table in the break room during lunch, her brow furrowed in concentration and golden curls flopping over her forehead as she pores over a stack of paperwork. She knows it's risky, knows they should keep their distance outside the safety of their locker room, but the magnetic pull she feels towards Hallie Hunter is just too strong to resist.

With a mischievous grin, Kaia saunters over to the table and slides onto the bench beside Hallie. "Hey, Lieutenant," she murmurs, her voice low and sultry. "Got a minute?"

Hallie's head snaps up, her eyes widening as she takes in Kaia's closeness. She quickly glances toward the open door, ensuring no one is within earshot, before whispering harshly, "Kaia, what are you doing? We can't be seen together like this."

But Kaia is undeterred, the lingering thrill of

their forbidden tryst coursing through her veins like a drug. She leans in even closer, her breath ghosting over Hallie's ear as she purrs, "I was just thinking, after yesterday, I owe you some attention... fancy meeting me in the locker room in five?"

A pink flush creeps up Hallie's neck as she scoots along the bench to put some distance between them.

"Absolutely not!" she hisses, her eyes darting around to the door once more.

"It's way too risky for us to just disappear in the middle of the day. What if someone saw us both go in there? If what we did becomes public knowledge, I could lose my job. We both could lose our jobs."

Kaia pouts, but she knows Hallie has a point. Still, she can't help but push, the desire to be alone with her consuming her every thought. With a bashful smile, she continues to tease her.

"Well then, Lieutenant, I guess you'll just have to take me out on a proper date if you want to spend any more *quality* time together."

Hallie pauses, her brow furrowed in thought, and chews on her cheek as she considers her response. Kaia holds her breath, terrified she may be making more of their connection than she should. But she can feel it; she knows Hallie wants her just as badly. Kaia can only hope that discretion at work is the only thing holding the lieutenant back.

Then, slowly, a smile spreads across Hallie's face.

"Okay," she finally says. "How about we go for a hike this weekend, just the two of us? I know a great spot with an amazing view. I go there sometimes to escape; the stars are incredible when you're away from the city pollution."

Kaia arches an eyebrow, a bolt of excitement zipping down her spine.

"A night beneath the stars for our first date, huh?" she drawls, her lips curling into a smirk. "My, my, how presumptuous of you, Lieutenant Hunter!" She punctuates her words with a playful wink, delighting in the way Hallie's cheeks flush an even deeper shade.

"What? No, I didn't mean—I just thought it would be nice to—" Hallie stammers.

But Kaia just giggles, cutting her off with a wave of her hand.

"I'm just teasing. It sounds romantic as fuck.

Besides… I already let you take advantage of me in the showers. I don't intend to play coy, now."

Hallie can't seem to suppress the smile tugging at the corners of her lips.

"You're incorrigible, you know that, Montgomery?" she murmurs, shaking her head. "But you've got yourself a date."

They both manage to relax into a comfortable routine over the following days, content in the shared knowledge that they can act freely once the weekend comes. Even during their one-on-one sessions, they maintain a professional demeanor, conscious that they could be spotted at any moment appearing too close.

By the time Friday rolls around, Kaia is wound tight with anticipation, practically skipping out the door after the final debriefing. Hallie watches her from where she leans against the desk at the front of the room, an obvious smirk spread across her sharp features.

"Big plans this weekend, Montgomery?"

"Nah, nothing too exciting, Lieutenant. Just happy to have some time to kick back," Kaia throws over her shoulder, relishing Hallie's scoffed laugh in response.

The following morning, Hallie pulls up

outside Kaia's apartment building in her sand-crusted truck, bright and early. Kaia can't help throwing sidelong glances her way throughout their drive beyond the city limits, her blood heating with every shameless perusal of Hallie's muscular frame exposed by her shorts and tank top.

"I'm so looking forward to a day of hiking with you under the desert sun," she jokes, pulling at the neck of her already damp t-shirt. "Making me sweat even on our day off. You must be some kind of crazy sadist. Or masochist, seeing as it's also your day off. Either way... crazy," she finishes with a shrug.

Hallie chuckles, the sound warm and rich as the stunning terrain surrounding them.

"Hey, a good firefighter never stops training!" she says with a grin. "Besides, my family used to hike all the time back home. It's in my blood."

They eventually pull into the sheltered parking lot Hallie had selected for the start of their trail. Hoisting their packs onto their backs, Kaia bites back a groan at the weight of the supplies, deter-mined as always to prove her strength to her unshakeable lieutenant.

The promised reward of a night with Hallie

under the stars was more than enough to persuade her to hike this trail ten times over.

Intrigued by her earlier comment, Kaia peppers Hallie with questions as they start along the trail, eager to learn more about her past. Hallie indulges her, sharing stories of her childhood adventures and the tight-knit family that raised her to pursue her dreams.

As they walk, Kaia can't help but steal glimpses of her date, admiring the way the sun glints off her golden hair, the way her muscles flex and ripple beneath her shining skin. The attraction between them is palpable, electric, and Kaia finds herself counting down the moments until they can relax in complete seclusion.

After a couple of hours of lighthearted conversation punctuated by stretches of slightly labored breathing, they reach Hallie's favorite lookout spot. Kaia's breath is taken from her completely as she surveys the flat ridge with a panoramic view of the desert valley below.

They work together to set up their small tent, Kaia settling into the comfortable rhythm of following Hallie's instructions. Every so often, their hands brush as they secure the poles, sending shivers down Kaia's spine.

As the sun begins to set, painting the sky in vivid golds and oranges, the two of them sit side-by-side at the edge of the ridge, their feet dangling over the ledge. The view is stunning, but Kaia finds herself more captivated by the woman beside her, the way the fading light dances across her features, softening them in a way Kaia has never seen before.

"I'm a little jealous, you know," Kaia admits quietly, after a long moment of silence spent looking out over the beautiful desert. "Of how close your family is. I wish I had that."

Hallie turns to look at her, her brow furrowed. "What do you mean?" she asks softly. "Aren't you close with your family?"

Kaia sighs, picking at a loose thread on her shorts. "Yes and no," she mumbles. "My mom and brothers are great; we've always been really tight. But my parents had a messy divorce when I was young."

She takes a deep breath before continuing, the words spilling out of her in the comfortable safety of Hallie's presence. "All my time with Dad was kinda tense after that, every other weekend. He was... Well, you already know how he feels about my career choices. He's always treated me so differently from my brothers. Made a point of constantly reminding me that I'm a girl, that I couldn't just follow everything they did."

Hallie reaches over and takes Kaia's hand, entwining their fingers.

"That must have been rough," she murmurs, her thumb stroking soothing circles over Kaia's knuckles. "He should be proud of everything you've achieved. But even if he isn't, I know your mom must be, and your brothers. I know it's easier said than done, but don't let his judgement drown out your own pride in yourself."

Kaia meets Hallie's eyes, seeing the empathy shining there, and has to swallow against the lump forming in her throat.

"Thank you. I could never have predicted in a million years that this would happen." She gestures between them, glancing down at their joined hands. "But, since that first day I walked into the station, all I've wanted to do is prove myself to you. To the one person I've met who truly understands what I'm going through and has beaten the odds to silence all the asshole men out there who doubted her."

Hallie smiles, giving Kaia's fingers a reassuring

squeeze. She leans in, her lips finding the rookie's for a soft, tender kiss.

"You'll show them all just like I did. You're doing it already," she whispers, brushing her nose against Kaia's before capturing her mouth again.

Kaia winds her arm around Hallie's neck, pulling her closer to deepen their kiss and clawing her fingers through the soft bristles of the back of her cropped hair. Hallie huffs a small chuckle, breaking away to pepper a line of kisses down Kaia's neck.

"We should lay out the bedrolls. You know... to watch the stars," she says, sucking at the skin where Kaia's neck meets her shoulder.

Kaia giggles and bats her away. "Don't leave any marks on me I'll have to explain to my boss."

They lay out their bedrolls side by side, a safe distance from the ridge, and Kaia can't stop herself from rattling off fire safety protocols in a robotic voice while Hallie expertly builds them a small campfire. Hallie laughs and playfully claps her hand over Kaia's mouth before pulling her down to the soft mats.

"Relax, rookie. I know what I'm doing. You really think I would risk an emergency callout when I've got you out here all to myself?"

Kaia shakes off Hallie's grip with a chuckle. "You make a good point, Lieutenant. That would make for a very awkward discovery if our entire crew showed up."

She stares up at Hallie as she hovers over her, her head resting on her fist while the other hand drifts down to caress the sliver of exposed skin at Kaia's waist. A simmering eagerness rises in Kaia's veins, days of restrained lust bubbling to the surface as she gazes into Hallie's sparkling eyes.

"I know you brought me here to see the stars," she breathes, pulling Hallie's mouth down to her own until their lips brush while she speaks. "But they'll be there all night, right?"

She feels Hallie's answering smirk against her lips before she kisses her, slow and languid while their tongues explore each other after all the time they've spent holding themselves back.

Before long, Kaia's arousal becomes too hot for her to bear. Hallie gasps a small yelp when Kaia flips her, pinning her to the bedroll as she settles herself between Hallie's legs. She's determined to repay every drop of pleasure Hallie drew out of her in the showers that day, her competitive streak dominating her as always.

Kaia's greedy hands push up Hallie's top while

she nips and laves at the sticky skin of her smooth stomach. They both succumb to lusty impatience as Hallie yanks her shirt over her head, unclasping her sports bra when Kaia kneels up to strip her own upper half.

A low moan rumbles through Hallie's chest while Kaia leans down to suck her nipple into her mouth, stroking the length of her thigh as she hitches Hallie's leg around her waist. Kaia kneads and pulls at Hallie's small breasts, alternating between the two with her mouth until Hallie is a writhing mess beneath her.

The triumph is an electric current, zinging through Kaia's muscles while she reduces the formidable lieutenant to putty in her hands. She can't help her smug smile as she rises to hover above Hallie, gazing into her hooded eyes as she reaches for the drawstring at the front of her shorts.

"In my professional opinion, these represent an unnecessary obstruction," Kaia quips, relishing Hallie's chuckle as she drags her shorts down her thighs, peeling off her panties at the same time.

"Well spotted, rookie. You must have been trained by a great lieutenant," she throws back, panting slightly. Hallie's breath hitches when Kaia strokes a lazy path through her glistening folds with her thumb, drinking in the sight of her naked body spread beneath her.

Leaning down to capture Hallie's lips again in a hungry, bruising kiss, Kaia plunges a finger inside her. It slips in so easily through the slickness gathered there, she quickly adds another, reassured by Hallie's shameless moans that she's stroking the spot that will bring her right to the edge.

But Kaia wants to draw this out, drive Hallie crazy with her fingers, her tongue, until she's desperate for release. Kissing her way back down Hallie's body, she slows the pumping of her fingers, withdrawing them completely to lick off the sweet musk of Hallie's arousal.

Humming her enjoyment at the heady taste, Kaia dips her head to lick a long stripe up through Hallie's labia before gently sucking at her clit. Her hips buck slightly as she groans in response, winding her fingers into Kaia's wild curls.

Kaia's touches are as reverent as they are forceful, basking in the unfamiliar power of having Hallie crumbling beneath her hungry kisses and bruising grasp on her quivering thighs. She worships Hallie's skin, licking and sucking and nibbling until a sharp yank at her scalp forces her to look up.

"What's with all the teasing?" Hallie demands breathlessly. "We may have all night, Kaia, but I was hoping to spend some of it between your legs. Not on my back being edged for hours on end."

Kaia chuckles, "You just can't help being the boss, can you?"

Hallie pulls her hair tighter, urging her to crawl up her body until they're nose to nose again.

"Get used to it, Montgomery," she murmurs and pulls her in for a quick kiss. "Now get those shorts off and come sit on my face. I want to taste you while you put those clever fingers back inside me, fucking me until I come. Don't make me wait any longer."

Kaia groans as she quickly obeys, peeling off her own shorts and damp underwear before turning to brace her knees either side of Hallie's head. The dominant tone of Hallie's commands is intoxicating, burning through her veins and throbbing in her own aching core.

She leans forward to plunge her hand back between Hallie's legs at the same time as Hallie's arms snake around her thighs, pulling her down until her lips meet Kaia's needy pussy.

The feeling is pure, sinful ecstasy. Kaia grinds her clit against Hallie's expert tongue, panting and mewling as she feels her climax building faster than ever. She gasps air, trying to focus on hooking her fingers enough to hit that perfect spot inside Hallie, while her eyes roll back in her head.

Kaia rubs the heel of her palm against Hallie's own swollen clit while she continues to pump her fingers in and out, certain she must be close as her hips buck in time with Kaia's punishing rhythm. Then all at once, Hallie tenses and clamps her lips around Kaia's clit, humming a long, low groan.

Kaia immediately folds forwards, forcing Hallie's thighs open as they try to clamp shut around her shuddering orgasm. Kaia licks and sucks at Hallie's pussy until the aftershocks subside, bracing her hands on the ground as Hallie's devouring tongue has her own legs trembling uncontrollably.

As her own orgasm barrels into her like a freight train, Kaia struggles not to collapse, the delicious spasms pulsing through her legs until they're practically jelly.

But Hallie doesn't stop, kneading greedy fingers into Kaia's ass cheeks as she continues feasting until the sensitivity becomes too much.

Kaia giggles and pants as she crawls forward on weak knees to escape Hallie's greedy lips.

"You're going to kill me," she huffs out, swinging her leg round until she can lie down beside Hallie, folding herself into her equally breathless companion's awaiting arms.

"Where's that infamous stamina, Montgomery?" Hallie quips through a wolfish grin. "I'm just getting started."

9

HALLIE

Hallie wakes to the soft morning light filtering through the tent's thin fabric. Beside her, Kaia sleeps peacefully, her dark curls splayed above her head, her face serene. For a little while, Hallie simply watches her, drinking in the sight like a parched traveler stumbling upon an oasis. There's a sense of contentment settling deep in her chest, a warm peace she's never experienced waking up beside previous girlfriends.

Is that what Kaia is? My girlfriend?

A creeping nervousness pinches at her chest. She has no clue how she would go about asking her. If she even should.

Whatever it is that has blossomed between

them is far from what Hallie expected, and she doesn't know how they could even make it work without risking their positions at the station.

As if she's sensed Hallie tensing, Kaia stirs, her eyelids blinking slowly as she wakes. Hallie reaches out, gently brushing a stray curl from Kaia's cheek, marveling at the softness of her lovely glowing brown skin.

"Morning," she whispers, her voice tender in the quiet of their secluded escape.

Kaia opens her eyes fully, a sleepy smile spreading across her full lips. Without a word, she leans in, capturing Hallie's mouth in a soft, languid kiss.

"Morning," she murmurs, her hand coming up to cup Hallie's cheek. Hallie melts into the touch, into the warmth of Kaia's body pressed against her own.

They stay like that for a while, trading gentle kisses and caresses, hands drifting across the curves and planes of each other's bodies. It's a different kind of passion than the sweaty tangling of the night before, but somehow far more intimate.

Hallie feels like she could stay here forever,

wrapped in Kaia's arms, the rest of the world and its problems left far beyond the arid desert.

But soon enough, the loud rumble of Hallie's stomach breaks the spell. Kaia throws her head back with a laugh, a bright, joyful sound that makes Hallie's heart skip a beat.

"How about breakfast?" she suggests, sitting up and stretching her arms above her head. Hallie watches, mesmerized, as the muscles in Kaia's back flex and ripple beneath her smooth skin.

They settle themselves on the ridge again, nibbling on their scant supply of protein bars and sipping coffee from a thermos. Kaia nudges Hallie's shoulder playfully.

"You know, I don't think we spent very much time admiring the stars last night," she teases, her eyes sparkling with mirth.

Hallie nearly chokes on her coffee, a warm blush spreading across her cheeks.

"Oh, really?" she sputters. "And whose fault is that?"

Kaia's grin widens. "Hey now, I didn't hear you complaining, Lieutenant."

Hallie huffs a low chuckle, the easy banter flowing between them feeling as natural as breathing. It's entirely new to her, this effortless connection. She's spent so long building walls, convincing herself she didn't need anyone, fueling her soul with pure ambition and independence. But with Kaia, those walls seem to be crumbling at an almost terrifying rate.

Once they've packed up the tent and started the hike back down the ridge, Hallie is firmly in her head. The two of them settle into a comfortable silence, and she takes the opportunity to try and sort through the swirling emotions that are starting to feel too big to fit inside her ribcage.

She can't help but keep stealing glances at Kaia, thinking about how easy it is to be with her, how she seems to understand and accept every part of her, even the parts that have always driven other women away.

Kaia recognizes the intense commitment Hallie has to her career. Hell, Kaia's own dedication could rival hers.

A creeping heat coils low in Hallie's stomach when her mind wanders to how Kaia also seems to enjoy her dominant side once they're naked together, her fiery demeanor banking ever so slightly when Hallie starts calling the shots.

"What are you smirking at?" Kaia's question snaps Hallie out of her silent musings.

"Huh? Oh, nothing. I was just remembering how much you liked taking orders last night."

Kaia scoffs, though the twitching in her cheeks makes it clear she's fighting back a smile.

"Only from you, Lieutenant. No one else."

They descend once more into their light-hearted banter, trekking at a leisurely pace beneath the morning sun. As they approach her waiting truck, a thought begins to take shape in Hallie's mind, a question she's been too afraid to ask herself in recent days.

Could Kaia be the one I've been holding out for? Could we be in this for the long run?

But even as the dream begins to take shape, Hallie feels a sense of unease tugging at the edges of her mind. She can't ignore the risk they're taking, that screwing it up could bring everything they've worked for crashing down around both of them.

The next few weeks pass in a blur of heated glances and sweaty nights. Whenever they can, Hallie and Kaia find ways to be together, whether it's a stolen kiss in the locker room or a long night in with takeout and action movies.

They're always careful at work, always looking over their shoulders, never getting too close where their crewmates might spot them. But even so, Hallie can't shake the growing sense of paranoia that comes with each passing day they have to hide their relationship.

Her fears rise to the surface with a vengeance one morning at a routine crew meeting. While all of their colleagues are gathered in the same room, Hallie notices a few sidelong glances and whispered remarks between a few of the rookies as they eye Kaia perched on the edge of a desk at her lieutenant's side.

Their crossed arms aren't even close to touching but, once she notices the looks they're getting, Hallie tries and fails to focus on the captain's speech.

Her mind is spinning with worst-case scenarios.

She imagines the rumors spreading like wildfire, the knowing glances and snide remarks. She sees herself losing the respect of her superiors, her crewmates, the authority she's worked so hard to earn.

Worst of all, she pictures Kaia's career going up in flames, all because her lieutenant couldn't keep her hands to herself.

After the meeting, Hallie marches towards her office, trying to calm her racing thoughts. That's when she hears it—a snippet of conversation between two of the rookies lingering in the hallway. "You've seen the way they look at each other in training. Think Montgomery is tryna fuck her way to the top?" one of them murmurs, his voice low.

"Maybe," his companion responds, "Hell, I might try it if I thought Hunter was into dick."

They both stride round the corner out of her sight, sniggering with every step. Clearly, they didn't think to check who was walking behind them.

Hallie's blood runs cold, fear gripping her lungs in a vice.

Desperate to quash the rumors before they can take root, Hallie makes a decision. She needs to be harder on Kaia in front of her fellow recruits, to create the illusion of distance between them. It's the only way she can think of to protect their careers, to keep their relationship from becoming a public spectacle.

With a heavy heart, Hallie squares her shoulders and heads towards the training ground, wishing she could have a moment to warn Kaia before launching her plan into action. She knows it won't be easy on her, knows that every harsh word and critical comment will feel like a knife twisting in her gut.

Hallie can only hope that Kaia will forgive her, once she has a chance to explain.

She strides out into the training yard, her heart pounding in her chest and a slight sweat spreading across her brow that isn't entirely down to the burning, Nevada sun. She spots Kaia standing slightly apart from the other recruits as usual.

For a moment, Hallie's resolve wavers.

She doesn't want to give the male rookies any more reasons to sneer at Kaia. Criticizing her publicly could tear down the hard-won respect she's steadily built over the past weeks of excelling in every training session.

But Hallie is convinced she has no other choice. She can't give any of them any more reason to think she praises Kaia's performance just because they like to take each other's clothes off behind closed doors.

Steeling herself for a tough morning, Hallie

claps her hands, drawing the attention of the group. "Alright, listen up!" she barks, her voice as sharp and commanding as always. "Today, we're going to be running drills on team communication and coordination. At this point you should be working together seamlessly, like a well-oiled machine. Understood?"

A chorus of "Yes, Lieutenant!" rings out across the yard.

Hallie nods, her jaw tight. "Good. Let's get started."

She divides the recruits into pairs, assigning each a series of tasks designed to test their ability to work together under pressure and communicate clearly. The first exercise involves navigating a makeshift maze, with one partner giving verbal directions to their blindfolded crewmate.

"Remember," Hallie calls out as the recruits stumble their way around obstacles, "clear, concise communication is key. Your partner's life is in your hands."

She watches Kaia like a hawk, her chest swelling with pride when she completes the exercise perfectly, both listening and instructing with admirable precision. Hallie opens her mouth to praise Kaia's guidance of her blindfolded partner, but quickly snaps it shut when she remembers she needs to be looking for an opportunity to tell Kaia off.

Next, the teams must work together to carry a heavy training mannequin through an obstacle course, simulating the challenges of maneuvering a victim or equipment in a real-life rescue.

"Keep the load steady!" Hallie shouts, watching as the rookies struggle to maintain their grip. "If you drop it, you start again from the beginning."

As the day wears on, Hallie commits to singling Kaia out at every turn. She criticizes her form, her speed, her decision-making, pushing her harder than she's ever pushed anyone before. Soon, her voice grows hoarse from shouting.

Kaia, for her part, takes it all in her stride, gritting her teeth and pushing through the pain, determined to prove herself, as always. But Hallie can see the confusion in her eyes. The hurt. The silent question hanging between them,

Why are you doing this to me?

Hallie's chest aches with every harsh word, every biting comment. She hates herself for what she feels she has to do, for the way she tears Kaia down in front of her team. For the first time in her career, Hallie starts to resent her role as the tough, uncompromising lieutenant.

The last drill of the day is a high-stakes simulation of a multi-level building fire. The recruits must work in teams to locate and evacuate trapped civilians, coordinating their efforts and maintaining constant communication throughout the operation.

Hallie watches closely as Kaia and her teammate make their way through the smoke-filled structure, calling out to each other as they search for survivors. For a moment, it seems like they might actually pull it off without a hitch.

But then, just as they're about to make their final exit, Kaia appears to disagree with her partner's instructions, ignoring his call and taking a wrong turn instead. The mistake costs them precious seconds in the race against the clock.

Hallie takes a deep, levelling breath before she storms over to Kaia as soon as the exercise is complete, her fists clenched at her sides.

"Montgomery, what the hell was that?" she demands, committing to her performance. "You nearly cost your team the whole damn scenario. Do you even want to be here? Because from where

I'm standing, it looks like you think you should be running the whole department."

Kaia's eyes flash with hurt, eyebrows drawn together in obvious confusion.

"Of course I want to be here," she snaps back, her voice trembling a little. "I've worked my ass off to be a part of this crew."

Hallie's heart clenches at the raw pain in Kaia's voice. She wants to reach out to her, to tell her that it's just an act, that she's sorry. But she can't. She can only pray that one harsh dressing-down is enough to convince the rest of the rookies that she isn't playing favorites.

Instead, she narrows her eyes and takes a step closer, her voice dropping to a low, menacing growl. "Then you better start acting like it. Because right now, you're not just letting yourself down. You're letting your team down. You're letting me down."

Kaia's eyes widen at Hallie's brutal words. For a moment, Hallie thinks she might break, thick lines of moisture gathering in those warm, brown eyes. But then, something shifts in Kaia's expression. Her jaw tightens, and her eyes harden with resolve.

"You've made your point, Lieutenant," she bites

back, her voice steady and calm. "It won't happen again."

Hallie blinks, taken aback by Kaia's sharp response. Before she can say another word, Kaia turns on her heel and storms off the training ground, leaving a stunned silence in her wake.

She can feel the eyes of the other recruits on her, can sense their confusion and unease as they shift on their feet, waiting to be dismissed. But she can't bring herself to care about whether her plan had the desired effect. All she can think about is Kaia, and the look of betrayal painted across her face before she'd turned away.

10

KAIA

Kaia storms into her apartment that evening, slamming the door behind her with a resounding bang. She throws her bag across the room in a violent rage and collapses onto the couch. Burying her face in her hands, she tries to calm the storm in her head, the humiliation and hurt coursing through her veins.

How could Hallie do that to her? After everything they'd shared with each other, Kaia thought she'd found someone who truly understood her. Understood what she spent every day fighting for. But apparently, she was wrong. Apparently, Hallie's position will always come first.

Her iron grip on her team, on her power, certainly came before her feelings for Kaia today.

Kaia's cell begins to buzz insistently in her back pocket, the sound muffled by the couch cushions. She fishes it out, glaring at the screen where Hallie's picture stares up at her.

Taunting her.

With a scoff, Kaia declines the call and tosses the phone aside.

"I thought we had something real," she mutters to herself, anger and confusion warring in her chest. "Well done, Kaia. You really misjudged that one."

The phone buzzes again and again, each vibration grating on Kaia's already-frayed nerves, but she ignores it every time. If Hallie thinks a phone call is going to fix anything between them, she's got another think coming.

An hour passes. Maybe two. Kaia doesn't care to check the time.

She just stays where she is on the couch, replaying each minute she's spent with Hallie over and over, wondering how they all led to that gut-wrenching exchange in training today.

It all flashes before Kaia's eyes like a living nightmare. The way Hallie singled her out time and time again. The smug look on the other rook-ies' faces as they watched her get torn apart. The sharp stab in her ribcage when she realized that maybe, just maybe, Hallie wasn't who she thought she was.

A sudden knock at the door startles Kaia out of her spiraling thoughts so violently, she almost jumps out of her skin. She ignores it at first, content to pretend she isn't home just to avoid speaking to anyone. But the knocking persists, growing louder with each passing second.

With a frustrated growl, Kaia drags herself off the couch and stomps to the door. Yanking it open, she's poised to tell whoever it is to leave her the hell alone. But the command dies on her tongue when she sees Hallie standing there, fist still raised as if she were prepared to keep knocking all night.

"What do you want?" she bites out through a clenched jaw.

"Kaia, I'm so sorry, please let me explain." Hallie's voice is soft and pleading, the sound so foreign it only makes Kaia angrier.

"Oh, now you want to talk?" she snaps, clenching the door handle like she might slam it shut at any moment. "Seemed to me like all you wanted to do today was yell at me."

She starts to close the door, but Hallie quickly puts a hand up to stop it.

"Kaia, please! I was an ass, okay? I know I messed up, just let me explain."

"Explain what exactly?" Kaia scoffs. "How you decided to throw me under the bus in front of the entire squad? And for what, huh? To remind everyone that you're the bitch in charge?"

Hallie winces at Kaia's harsh words, but she refuses to back down.

"It wasn't like that. Come on, how can you think I would do that to you?" She takes a step closer to the doorway. "Please just let me in. I don't want to do this in the hall."

Kaia hesitates for a moment, the pleading in Hallie's glistening, blue eyes making her second guess her anger. This is the side of Hallie that she's only ever seen in their moments alone together, when the mask of the fierce lieutenant slips away. At last, with a heavy sigh, she steps aside, ready to hear Hallie's explanation at the very least.

The two of them stride into the living room, the tension thick and suffocating in the small space. Kaia crosses her arms over her chest, glaring at Hallie expectantly.

"Well?" she demands, raising an eyebrow. "You wanted to explain. So, start talking."

Hallie takes a deep breath.

"I overheard a couple of the rookies talking after the meeting this morning." Her words tumble out in a garbled rush. "Well, they were looking at us first—in the meeting, I mean—and I thought something was up."

Hallie begins pacing, nervously wringing her hands and struggling to make eye contact. Kaia tries not to gape; she's never seen this fearsome woman crumble like this.

"And then I heard them talking. And they were making crude jokes about whether you were trying to fuck your way to the top. I just—I panicked!" She spins on her heel then, reaching out to Kaia and then pulling her hands back again as if she's not confident Kaia would let **her** hold her right now.

"I thought..." Hallie's mouth opens and closes a few times, as if she's struggling to get the last part out. "I thought if I came down hard on you, if I made it seem like I didn't even like you... then, I could kill the rumors and we'd stay a secret."

Kaia's chest tightens, the hurt and the anger warring for dominance against the part of her heart that understands exactly what Hallie was trying to do.

"Why didn't you say something?" she breathes. "We could have come up with a plan together. Instead, you made me look like an incompetent idiot in front of the whole team."

Hallie claws her fingers through her messy, golden curls, pure anguish written across her face. "I know, it was stupid," she admits. "I just... I've worked my whole life to get to where I am. If word got out that I was sleeping with a recruit... it could... it would ruin my shot at becoming captain."

At that, Kaia huffs a bitter laugh, shaking her head. "Wow. So, that's what this is all about? Can't have a dirty secret hurt your precious career?" She throws her hands in the air and steps back, needing to put as much distance between them as possible.

"And what about me, Hallie? What about my career, huh? The guys on that team are just itching for a reason to get me booted. You made me look like an incapable child!"

"Kaia, please," Hallie begs, her voice cracking slightly. "I never meant to hurt you. I figured I could just explain afterwards. I made a mistake; I see that now."

"A mistake? Is that what you call it? Because from where I'm standing, it looks like you made a choice. Your career over me, Lieutenant Hunter."

Hallie shakes her head, her eyes starting to glisten on the brink of tears. "No, that's not true. My career would have been hurt, sure. But I can take a hit. Yours has just begun, Kaia, you wouldn't be able to come back from that kind of scandal." She takes a step forward, reaching for Kaia again. "I wanted to protect you too. I wanted to protect us both."

Kaia turns away, wrapping her arms around herself and squeezing, as if she could physically hold herself together. "I want to believe you," she says in a small, timid voice. "I want to believe that you won't chuck me away the minute things get too real."

Hallie comes to rest a warm hand on Kaia's shoulder. "They're already real for me, Kaia."

Kaia closes her eyes and exhales a shuddering breath. She had needed to hear those words from Hallie, to believe that everything she thought was between them wasn't one-sided.

"You mean that?" she murmurs, turning back

to face her. "This is... this is something real for you?"

"Oh, baby," Hallie sighs, bringing both hands up to cup Kaia's face. "I wouldn't be here if it wasn't. I'm sorry for fucking it up." She plants a soft kiss on the end of Kaia's nose and whispers, "I would crawl on my knees just to convince you of how much you mean to me."

Kaia giggles, overwhelmed with the roller-coaster of emotions this day has brought her, she flops her head forward to nuzzle into the side of Hallie's neck.

"I guess I could forgive you," she murmurs. "But I'm really not opposed to the whole on-your-knees-thing. You know... if that's still on the table."

A low chuckle rumbles through Hallie's chest. She snakes her fingers through Kaia's and leads her to the bedroom, stopping just as the backs of Kaia's calves hit the edge of the mattress.

"Let's get you naked, baby," Hallie whispers against Kaia's neck while she hooks her thumbs into the waistband of her sweatpants. "I have some groveling to do."

Kaia lets her head loll back with a groan before hurriedly peeling her tank top and sports bra over her head. Hallie is already sinking to her knees, dragging Kaia's panties down with her sweats and waiting there until she steps out of them.

Once Kaia is completely bare, Hallie peppers a trail of gentle kisses up each of her thighs, all the while staring up at her beneath hooded eyes.

"Do you like it when I'm on my knees for you?" Hallie murmurs, stroking her fingertips up the backs of Kaia's legs and leaving goosebumps in their wake.

"You have no idea," Kaia moans, raking her fingers through Hallie's unruly mop of cropped curls.

"Lie down, baby. Let me show you how sorry I am."

Kaia obeys, even with Hallie on her knees, she relishes the soft command, the warm safety of their usual dynamic.

Her toes curl in the plush carpet as Hallie begins worshipping her with her tongue, laving and sucking until Kaia's thighs start to quiver.

But it isn't enough.

Kaia pushes up on her elbows, locking eyes with an expectant Hallie.

"I want you to fuck me. Fuck me hard until I forget that I'm mad at you."

Hallie's answering chuckle sends a delicious

vibration through Kaia's core as her lips remain clamped around her throbbing clit. She releases it after a long, drawn-out suck that has the rookie's eyes rolling to the back of her head.

"As you wish," she answers, rising to a standing position and tearing off her own clothes.

Kaia scoots further up the bed, turning onto all fours in a clear demonstration of exactly how she wants Hallie to make it up to her. She watches in delicious anticipation as Hallie opens the night-stand, pulling out the harness and dildo she had brought round the previous week.

As Hallie gets fastened, Kaia has to swallow the urge to drool, spreading her knees further apart and stroking a finger through her own slick folds as she waits impatiently.

Hallie rounds the back of the bed and settles herself between Kaia's legs. She slaps Kaia's hand away from her clit and then lands another blow on her ass for good measure. Kaia keens and rocks back, desperate for Hallie to fill her up as soon as possible.

But Hallie moves slow and teasing, brushing the head of the dildo through Kaia's lips and spreading her gathering arousal.

"So wet for me," Hallie says in a quietly reverent tone.

She kneads Kaia's ass with her other hand, caressing and spreading her open as she pushes slowly inside her, inch by inch.

Kaia moans and pushes back more forcefully this time, greedily chasing the fullness Hallie is taking her sweet time to give her. Her impatience earns her another sharp spank, and Kaia bites down on her lower lip, groaning and gasping as Hallie finally picks up the pace.

The punishing rhythm Hallie sets is overwhelming, hitting that perfect spot inside Kaia that turns her legs liquid and sends ripples of pleasure right to her fingertips. She closes her eyes and succumbs to the fog of blissful lust that clouds her brain.

Just for that moment of pure, warm surrender, she forgets everything that Hallie had snapped at her today, she forgets how hurt she was, how angry.

Hell, as Hallie pounds into her over and over, Kaia starts to forget her own name.

Kaia hears her own moans louder than ever. She is lost in the exquisite feeling of Hallie fucking her hard as Hallie's hand grips her hip roughly.

Kaia's ass is in the air and her face seeks out the comfort of the pillow.

Suddenly, without warning, Hallie reaches forward and winds her fingers into Kaia's hair, yanking her upright and flush against her sweat-slicked body.

Kaia yelps, the new angle hitting her G spot and making her legs shake uncontrollably as she leans back against Hallie's strong torso.

Hallie caresses and worships her, bringing a hand up to knead and pull roughly at one of Kaia's nipples while she snakes the other round to stroke rapid circles around her throbbing clit.

All the while she bites and sucks at Kaia's neck and shoulder, fucking into her while she worships as much of her skin as she can reach.

It takes barely a minute for Kaia to completely come undone, her climax building deliciously low in her core before exploding all at once, sending a white haze across her vision.

She feels herself gush hot and wet across Hallie's thighs.

It's all she can do to grasp at Hallie's strong arms as she strokes and thrusts through Kaia's orgasm until she's totally spent. As she eventually slows, Kaia sags slightly, confident that Hallie won't drop her while she pants and trembles.

"Was that enough groveling for you, baby?" Hallie whispers against Kaia's sticky neck.

For a moment, Kaia can't offer anything more than a contented moan.

She sighs and blinks slowly, perfectly satisfied and wrapped in Hallie's warm embrace.

"Maybe," she eventually exhales. "Give me a couple of minutes and I'm sure I'll be ready to go again. Tell me you planned to stay over tonight."

Hallie huffs a quiet laugh, gently easing Kaia to the mattress and pulling out of her thoroughly pleased pussy.

"I wouldn't dream of leaving so soon."

11

HALLIE

Hallie strides into the station the next morning with a slight bounce in her step and a smile playing on her lips. Kaia's forgiveness—and the hours they spent tangled in a mess of sweaty limbs afterwards—last night has made her feel more secure in their relationship than any she's been in before.

They had had their first real fight and have come out the other side stronger than ever.

Hallie greets Art warmly as she joins him for their first morning coffee together in weeks, having promised Kaia that they could skip one-on-one training for the day.

Just as she's raising her mug to her lips for that first, searing sip, the alarm blares, its shrill tone echoing throughout the entire station. Hallie sprints after Art as they both rush out to the garage, her good mood evaporating as she takes in the grim faces of her fellow firefighters.

"We have a major emergency at the Desert Oasis Resort," Captain Hewitt announces in his booming voice. "The blaze has engulfed the twenty-fifth floor of the western high-rise. Numerous civilians suspected trapped inside. Let's move people, we need to act fast."

Hallie hauls herself into an engine, conducting a silent head count of her crew and making brief but loaded eye contact with Kaia.

The Desert Oasis is a mammoth resort, with a complex layout and capacity for hundreds of guests in the western high-rise alone. This is going to be a monumental operation; they can't afford any mistakes. She can only hope that Kaia under-stands everything she is trying to say in that look.

Please, stay alert. Please, stay with your team. Please, stay safe.

Kaia gives her a small nod, eyes blazing with that familiar determination, before turning away. Hallie understands her response, they can't afford to worry about each other today, they have to be one hundred percent focused.

When their convoy of engines pulls up at the resort, Hallie blanches at little at the sight. Even with all her years of disaster experience, it never gets easier to face a lethal crisis like this head-on.

Thick, black smoke billows from the upper floors, darkening the sky, and the sound of screams and shattering glass fills the air. She leaps out of the truck without giving herself even half a second to feel afraid, bellowing instructions to her crew.

"Alright, listen up! We're splitting into containment and evac! Squad 3 you're on evac with me, keep your ears open, I'm running comms from the ground!"

The rookies nod, jaws set beneath their helmets. Hallie can't help the pang of fear that pierces her gut as Kaia joins her teammates activating her breathing apparatus and readying to enter the blazing tower. She knows Kaia is a capable firefighter, and fiercely brave, but the thought of her in danger still sends an icy chill down the lieutenant's spine.

As the minutes tick by, Hallie monitors the radio chatter, systematically guiding her squad through their evacuation operation on the upper floors. So far, it's going smoothly, but the fire is spreading fast, and they're running out of time before the structure becomes too unstable for the rescue team to stay inside.

Then Hallie's worst fear is realized.

A distressed call out from Cochran crackles over the radio. "Lieutenant, we have a problem. Montgomery has separated from the group."

Hallie's chest seizes as she struggles to choke down a breath. She immediately barks into her radio, her voice hoarse with tension, "Montgomery, return to your squad immediately! You have not been authorized to move into any area alone."

A few, agonizing seconds pass where Hallie hears nothing but static, before Kaia's response comes through, breathless but controlled. "Negative, Lieutenant. We're moving too slowly. Civilians are running out of time before this whole place comes down. I can speed up the rescue by tackling twenty-eight alone."

The lieutenant's grip tightens so much on her radio, it's a wonder it doesn't crush into pieces.

She knows Kaia is right, time is against them, but branching off alone in this kind of disaster zone is against every bit of protocol Hallie has drilled into her rookies since the day they stepped foot on her training ground.

"Dammit, Kaia," she mutters under her breath, before raising the radio back to her lips. "Cochran, Richards! Assist Montgomery on the twenty-eighth floor, she shouldn't be up there alone."

"No can do, Lieutenant," Cochran's sharp response has a churning nausea growing in Hallie's gut. "Twenty-seven isn't clear yet, we have civilians in tow. We have to get them out first."

Before the lieutenant has a chance to respond, Kaia's voice rings out again, this time noticeably strained. "Structural damage on the east side of twenty-eight. Do not attempt rescue, it's too unstable. No survivors found."

Hallie's stomach falls straight through her feet. "Get clear, Montgomery! Evac is winding down."

"I'm working on it, Boss."

The lieutenant's fierce resolve begins to well and truly crumble. Kaia sounds like she's struggling more than she's letting on.

And her crewmates are making their way down twenty-seven floors to the ground, getting further away from her with every passing second.

"Montgomery, confirm self-evac, now!"

"Negative, Lieutenant." Kaia's response is the most feeble Hallie's ever heard her voice. "Obstructed descent. I'm trying to clear a path."

Hallie clenches her eyes closed against rapidly encroaching tears. Every instinct in her body is screaming at her to rush in, to save the woman she's grown to care about so deeply, even when her recklessness infuriates her beyond measure.

But the lieutenant knows the risks. The tower is on the verge of collapse, she would never authorize re-entry for any other members of her squad.

She opens her eyes again to assess the sight before her, torn between everything she knows as a veteran firefighter and everything she feels as Kaia's partner.

Because that's what she is now. Her partner. Inside the department and out.

In the end, there's no choice to make. Hallie throws on her own breathing apparatus and sprints towards the building, alerting her team on the radio to complete their civilian evacuations and immediately join the containment squads. They had to put out this blaze.

The heat grows more overwhelming with every level Hallie races up the service staircase. The damage appears to be less severe on this side of the tower, but she knows what she'll be up against once she tries to navigate to the side of the twenty-eighth floor where Kaia is trapped.

Every muscle in Hallie's body screams at her as she keeps climbing and climbing.

She clutches at her breathing apparatus and gasps through a few deep inhales before attempting to radio Kaia again.

"Montgomery, report!"

"Ceiling cave-in meets collapsing floor. It's quite the circus up here, Lieutenant. I'm making my way across as fast as I can. Stand by."

Hallie bites back a sob. Kaia should have waited for her entire team's assessment of the integrity of the higher floor before rushing in alone.

"I'm coming, baby," she whispers to herself, clambering up more steps with renewed vigor.

Finally, Hallie reaches the twenty-eighth floor, forcing her way through the service door to encounter the disastrous reality of what's left of it.

She immediately spots Kaia, maybe twenty feet away, maneuvering too slowly across the obstacle course of exposed steel beams and crumbling plaster from all sides. The lieutenant assesses the expanse with sharp eyes, weighing their painfully limited options.

Just then, her gaze snags on a gaping hole in

the floor between them, on a half-collapsed bed visible from the floor below.

"Kaia, you'll have to jump!" she shouts across the roar of flames and fire hoses. "I'll head down to twenty-seven and pull you out."

Kaia raises her head beneath her helmet, her face too obscured for Hallie to make out if she's surprised to see her. She hesitates, glancing down to the floor below and then back to her formidable lieutenant.

She doesn't move.

"Kaia! You have to trust me! I won't leave you here."

The smallest sigh of relief escapes Hallie's lips when Kaia finally gives her a timid nod. She barrels back through the door she came through and leaps down a flight of stairs, 3 steps at a time.

When she bursts through the service door on the floor below, Hallie can only just make out Kaia's figure through the steadily rising smoke. She sprints towards the mattress and yanks it towards her, desperate to find an area of floor that might bear the weight of Kaia's descent.

Ready in her position, she radios Kaia, terribly aware that they may soon run out of seconds before they can kiss their shot at escaping goodbye.

"Now, Kaia! Jump now! I've got you."

Kaia hesitates for another agonizing moment until a flaming beam crashes down behind her, forcing her to lurch forward.

If she doesn't move now, it'll be too late.

"Come on, baby," Hallie pleads under her breath.

Then Kaia jumps, hurtling through the air as ash and debris flutter around her.

She lands on her hands and knees in the center of the sagging mattress. Hallie immediately reaches out to grab her arm, hoisting her across the trembling floor and towards the relative safety of the service exit.

When they both collapse in front of the door, they pant for a few seconds in tense silence.

Suddenly, a deafening creak pierces Hallie's eardrums and her stinging eyes widen in pure terror as more of the ceiling starts to give way. She doesn't stop to think as she throws her body over Kaia's, just as huge chunks of plaster rain down from above.

The impact knocks the wind from Hallie

completely, clanging through her teeth and battering her spine and legs with brutal force.

Kaia starts to crawl backwards, dragging her lieutenant with her until they make it through the door to stairs. Without a word, she pulls Hallie to her feet and throws her arm over her shoulders, supporting her trembling weight as they begin their hurried descent to the exit.

Each floor passes with a dizzying blur. It's all Hallie can do to keep moving, keep breathing through the acrid, soot-laden air that gets sightly clearer the closer they make it to the ground.

At last, they tear through the exit, neither of them daring to slow their pace until they make it to the engines a hundred yards from the building.

They both collapse forward and heave, hands braced on their knees as they try to choke down air. The pure adrenaline coursing through Hallie's veins seems to collect like a swirling vice around her stomach. But there's nothing in there for her to throw up.

She removes her helmet tossing it to the ground as she struggles to right herself. Looking up, she catches sight of Kaia's soot-smeared face, her dark eyes boring into Hallie's with unrestrained rage.

Before Hallie can cough up the words to ask why Kaia looks so angry, they're each whisked away by paramedics for check ups and fitted with oxygen masks at different ambulances.

Once she's cleared by the medics, the lieutenant makes it back to her rig, shocked to find Kaia furiously pacing with her arms crossed tightly across her chest. The absence of her jacket reveals Kaia's sweat-slicked arms are marred by various scrapes and bruises. Hallie's heart clenches at the sight of the bandages encasing one of her hands as well as her bicep.

Kaia glances up at Hallie's approaching, instantly storming over to her and wrapping her fingers around her shoulders in a bruising grip.

"What the fuck was that? Why did you come up there?" she hisses, shaking Hallie slightly in her grasp.

"What do you mean? I had to get you out," Hallie answers, bewildered by Kaia's demeanor.

"You should have left me, dammit! Christ, Hallie, what about protocol? You could have died trying to reach me!"

"Protocol?" the lieutenant spits back. "You want to talk to me about protocol? The only reason I had to come and save you in the first place is because you abandoned your fucking squad!"

Their hushed argument is beginning to draw an audience as more of their crewmates return to the engines, the remainder of the evac teams relieved of their duties.

"Drop whatever this is and get your ass on the rig, Kaia. I won't be snapped at by a rookie in the middle of a live operation."

Kaia chews her cheek, the ticking muscle in her jaw indicating to Hallie that she's biting back a retort. But she eventually strides away, hauling herself into their engine without a second glance at her perplexed lieutenant.

Hallie stays on sight to oversee the containment squads until the inferno is completely extinguished and the relevant city departments have arrived to determine how they're going to safely bring down the teetering, burnt out structure.

By the time she makes it back to the station, she has almost completely forgotten Kaia's outburst. That is, until she enters their locker room and finds her pacing again, glaring at the ground as if it's personally offended her.

"What's going on?" Hallie asks calmly, just

overwhelmed with relief that they both made it through the day alive and unharmed.

"I'm losing my mind, that's what's going on! You put your life at risk to save me. You can't do that, Hallie! You're supposed to be Queen-fucking-Protocol! How could you just chuck that away and run right into a crumbling high-rise?"

"Why?" Hallie grits out through clenched teeth. "Maybe because my fucking *girlfriend* got herself trapped when she *ignored* orders to stick with her squad!"

"Well, you should have left me to deal with my own choices!" Kaia snaps back. "Not made me almost responsible for your death."

They stare at each other, almost panting with restraint as they try to keep their furious tones hushed within the privacy of their women-only space.

"You don't get to make your stupid choices my problem, Kaia. I saved your life because I couldn't bear to lose you," Hallie rasps around the rising lump in her throat. "But I'm getting tired of trying to reign in your reckless instincts. I've done everything I can to teach you and you still barrel in, guns blazing, without a second thought for your squad or your own safety."

Kaia's eyes widen at Hallie's admission, shame darkening her cheeks as she drops her gaze to the ground.

"I was trying to give my all to the rescue. I was sure we could be doing more," she mumbles in the direction of her feet.

Hallie heaves a deep sigh, though it quivers in her chest as she tries desperately to hold back tears. "I know you were, Kaia. Your drive and your bravery are admirable, incredible even. But you don't know everything. And a lone wolf will never belong on my squad."

"What are you saying?" Kaia's face snaps up, panic stricken.

"I'm saying you better fall in line or I'm recommending your transfer to another station," the lieutenant responds. "And I think it's best for both of us if we end our relationship now, before we both get hurt."

Hallie inhales a shuddering breath as the first tear breaks free and snakes down her cheek. The shock and hurt in Kaia's face is a kick in the gut she struggles to take.

Kaia just gapes at her, clearly lost for words at the direction their argument is taking.

"You—you're breaking up with me? Because I ignored an order?"

"No, Kaia. I'm ending this because we should have never started it in the first place." Hallie tries to swallow around the emotions that are slicing her up from the inside, fighting to voice her decision in a more level tone.

"You're right, I could have died today because I was so desperate to get you out of there. We can't afford to be distracted by our feelings when lives are at stake."

She grabs her bag from her locker, deciding she'd rather drive home covered in the grime of today's disaster than stay in this room with Kaia for another second.

The devastation would crush her in seconds, and she'd take it all back.

"I'm sorry, Kaia," she chokes out, turning to grip the door handle with shaking fingers. "We'll just have to act like none of this ever happened. It's safer for both of us that way."

Without daring to glance back, she strides from the locker room.

Somehow managing to make it the entire drive home before breaking down, Hallie pushes open her apartment door in a daze. Only when she's closed it behind her and turned the lock does her composure finally crack. She collapses to the floor in her hallway as silent tears stream unbidden down past her clenched jaw.

12

KAIA

Not trusting herself to drive, Kaia walks the five miles back to her apartment. The world around her blurs into a hazy smear of streetlights and traffic sounds, muted and distant as if she's underwater. Her mind is just stuck on a loop, replaying those devastating words over and over until they're chiseled on the inside of her skull.

We'll just have to act like none of this ever happened.

The finality she heard in Hallie's voice weighs on Kaia's every step like a ball and chain. The distance in the lieutenant's eyes as she'd turned and walked away, leaving Kaia shattered in her wake. It's ironic, Kaia thinks to herself bitterly, that the woman who'd made her feel more alive than ever is now the source of a pain so sharp, it steals the breath from her lungs.

The sun has long since set by the time Kaia makes it home. Closing the door and leaning heavily against it, the weight of the day comes crashing down on her. The adrenaline that had sustained her through the harrowing call out and the confrontation with Hallie is gone now, leaving her hollow and aching. Slowly, she drags her feet to her bedroom, collapsing onto her bed and pulling her knees to her chest as if she can physically hold herself together.

But it's no use.

Harsh sobs wrack her frame as Kaia finally allows herself to fall apart, to feel the full magnitude of the past twelve hours. Kaia's chest constricts painfully as the reality of it all slams into her with the force of a speeding engine.

Her blazing anger, her reckless defiance, it was all fueled by the sheer terror of watching Hallie risk her own life to save Kaia's. The thought of losing her, of being the reason her lieutenant never made it out of that crumbling tower, it had clouded Kaia's vision with a red haze.

"Why did I have to lash out like that?" Kaia

whispers into the silence of her room, her voice raw and thick with tears.

Wiping at her eyes with trembling hands, Kaia fishes her phone out of her pocket. Fingers shaking, she pulls up Hallie's contact and hits the call button before she can secondguess herself.

The phone rings once, twice, three times. Each unanswered trill is like a knife to Kaia's heart, twisting deeper with every passing second. She starts to pace the length of her apartment, phone pressed to her ear hard enough to hurt.

"Pick up, Hallie. Come on," she pleads under her breath. "It can't end like this."

But the ringing eventually gives way to Hallie's curt, professional voicemail message. There's a beep, and then silence, expectant and suffocating. Kaia takes a shuddering breath, trying to compose herself enough to speak.

"Hallie, I'm sorry," she begins, hating the way her voice cracks. "Please, can we just talk about this? I know I was an idiot. I never meant to put you in danger. You mean too much to me to throw this away. Just...call me back. Please."

She ends the call and sinks onto the couch, staring at the phone in her hand as if she can will it to ring through desperation alone. Minutes tick by, each one an eternity as Kaia waits for a response that doesn't come. Hope soon gives way to a gnawing dread, cold tendrils of fear wrapping around her chest with every moment that passes and Hallie's name doesn't appear.

How long she sits there, eyes glued to the dark screen, Kaia doesn't know. Eventually, her phone chimes with an incoming text, startling Kaia so badly she nearly drops it. But as her eyes scan the words on the screen, Kaia feels the last, fragile embers of hope gutter and die in the darkness of her unlit sitting room.

I meant what I said. We need to focus on our careers right now, not let our feelings cloud our judgment on the job. It's better this way. See you at work.

The message is like a punch to the gut, cold and impersonal. Kaia stares and stares at it until the words blur together, disbelief and devastation warring for dominance in her heavy head. After everything they'd been through, all the moments of tenderness and passion, the whispered confessions in the dark, Hallie is really choosing her career over what they had?

A strangled sob tears from Kaia's throat, the phone slipping from her fingers and tumbling to the carpet. She curls in on herself, arms wrapped around her middle as she rocks back and forth. Hot tears spill down her cheeks, soaking into her sweatshirt as Kaia cries until her throat is raw and her eyes are swollen.

Exhaustion pulls her down to the couch cushions, the deep, bone-weary kind that only comes from heartbreak. Kaia doesn't fight it, doesn't have the strength to do anything but succumb to the oblivion of sleep. As her eyes slip closed, a final, devastating thought drifts through her mind like acrid smoke.

I've lost her. And it's all my fault.

The next morning, Kaia drags herself into the station, feeling like a husk of her former self. She moves on autopilot, going through the motions of her routine without really noticing anything around her. It's as if she's watching herself from a distance, puppeteering her own movements without actually being present in her own body.

She's just finished filling her coffee mug in the break room, staring blankly into the steaming depths as if they hold the answers to her misery, when a voice startles her out of her daze.

"Hey, Montgomery. Got a minute?"

Kaia turns to see Richards leaning against the counter, her fellow rookie's expression uncharacteristically somber. Instantly, she feels her defenses slam into place, her spine stiffening as she braces for the inevitable jab or snide remark.

"What do you want, Richards?" she asks warily, her fingers reflexively tightening around her coffee mug.

But he just holds up his hands, his eyes sincere as he meets her gaze.

"I come in peace," he says calmly. "I just wanted to say that I'm sorry about what happened at the resort. We should've had your back up there. That... that was some real shit."

Kaia blinks, taken aback by the genuine remorse in his voice. Of all the things she'd expected him to say, an apology was definitely not one of them.

Richards takes a step closer, his voice low and earnest. "Look, I know we've given you a hard time. But at the end of the day, we're a team. We need to trust each other if we're gonna make it in this job."

Kaia nods slowly, the words sinking in like a balm to her battered ego. She takes a deep breath, shoulders sagging as the weight of her own mistakes settles heavily on her.

"You're right," she admits quietly. "I-I need to

do better at being a team player too. No more lone wolf crap."

He grins at that, clapping her on the shoulder. "We all have our own shit to fix, it seems. Now come on, we've got drills to crush." He jerks his head towards the door, a clear invitation.

Kaia feels a small smile tug at the corners of her mouth, a flicker of warmth kindling in her chest in the face of his olive branch. She downs half of her coffee in one gulp before setting her mug down and following him out to the training ground, determination settling over her like a second skin. If she can't win back Hallie's heart, at least she can to prove her lieutenant—and herself —that she can be a valuable asset to this team.

But her resolve is tested the moment she steps out onto the tarmac and sees Hallie standing at the front of the assembled crew, her presence as commanding as ever. Kaia's heart clenches painfully at the sight of her, so close and yet so distant compared to weeks past. It takes every ounce of her strength not to let the hurt show on her face, to maintain the mask of calm profession-alism even as her insides twist themselves into knots.

"Listen up!" Hallie calls out, her voice ringing

with that familiar authority. "Today we're practicing rapid intervention. You'll each take turns as the firefighter down, trusting your teammate to get you out. Pair up."

Kaia feels a jolt of the usual unease at the prospect of having to work alongside one of the guys, but then Richards catches her eye, tilting his head in a silent question. *Partners?*

Relief washes over her immediately and Kaia nods, grateful to not be sneered at as she falls into line beside him. As Hallie goes over the drill, Kaia forces herself to focus on the task at hand, pushing aside the tumultuous emotions threatening to overwhelm her.

She can do this. Hallie is just the boss now.

The session is grueling as usual, both physically and mentally, but Kaia throws herself into it with everything she has. After the mess she got herself into yesterday, she has to prove that she can be a dependable teammate, that she's worthy of the trust being placed in her. She and Richards work seamlessly, communicating clearly and efficiently as they take turns playing the downed firefighter and the rescuer in various scenarios.

Throughout the entire morning, Kaia feels the weight of Hallie's gaze on her, watching her every move with critical eyes. It's a struggle not to let her emotions show, to keep her movements precise and her mind focused. But even as she pushes herself to her limits, Kaia can't shake the torture of being in Hallie's presence, the unspoken tension that crackles between them like a live wire.

Finally, the drills come to an end, and Kaia is left panting and sweat-drenched, her muscles burning with exertion. She braces for the lieutenant's final assessment, steeling herself for the cold professionalism she knows is coming.

"Good work, you two," Hallie says flatly, her face an impassive mask as she looks between Kaia and her partner.

There's no warmth in her voice, no hint of the affection that once colored her face when she praised Kaia. It's as if nothing ever happened between them, as if all that time they shared was nothing more than a figment of Kaia's imagination.

The heartbreak is like a physical thing, a vise around Kaia's chest that threatens to squeeze the life out of her. She swallows hard, fighting back the sudden sting of tears as she nods stiffly. This is how it's going to be from now on, she reminds herself, even as every fiber of her being seems to crumble where she stands.

Hallie doesn't want her anymore.

As the crew begins to disperse for lunch, Richards jogs over to Kaia, a grin on his face as he wipes the sweat from his pale brow.

"Hey, a bunch of us are grabbing drinks tonight," he huffs, slightly out of breath. "You should come, bond with the crew outside the station for once."

Kaia hesitates, her gaze drifting over to where Hallie is marching back towards her office. The thought of trying to be sociable, to pretend like everything is normal when her entire world has been turned upside down, is almost more than she can handle. She starts to shake her head, a weak excuse forming on her lips, but Richards beats her to it.

"C'mon, Kaia," he presses. "You're part of this crew same as any of us, and I swear we're not all that bad. One drink, that's all I'm asking."

Kaia sighs deeply, looking down at her feet as she toes the ground. She has a feeling Richards won't let it go very easily. And truth be told, the thought of going back to her empty apartment, to the echoes of Hallie's presence that linger in every corner, is suddenly suffocating.

"Alright, Richards," she relents, a wry smile tugging at her mouth. "One drink."

His grin widens as he claps her on the shoulder.

"Atta girl. Meet us at Murphy's at 8. And Kaia? Lose the last name basis crap. We're friends now. Call me Adam."

With that, he jogs off towards the guys' locker room, leaving Kaia to shake her head in bemusement. She doesn't know if she'd call them friends just yet, but perhaps a clean slate with this crew is exactly what she needs right now.

Hours later, Kaia pushes through the door of Murphy's Bar, the low thrum of music and chatter washing over her. She spots her crewmates gathered around one end of the bar, their laughter and easy camaraderie a stark contrast to the sidelong glances and sniggering she's become accustomed to since starting at Fire Station 3.

"Kaia!" Adam calls out, waving her over with a grin. "Glad you could make it. Get over here, Finn's buying the first round."

Kaia weaves her way through the crowd, pasting on an easy smile as she joins them. The guys are rowdy and boisterous, reminding her instantly of her older brothers as they clink glasses and chug beers. Kaia forces herself to laugh along, to join in the easy banter even as her gaze keeps wandering to the door, half-hoping and half-dreading that Hallie might walk through at any moment.

But as the night wears on and the alcohol starts to loosen the knot in her chest, Kaia feels herself start to relax at last. She finds herself trading stories and jokes with her fellow rookies, reveling in the way they include her so effortlessly, as if she's always been one of them.

"Gotta admit, Montgomery," Finn Cochran slurs at one point, raising his glass in a salute. "You're not so bad. To our sister in arms!"

"Hear, hear!" the others cheer, sloshing their drinks slightly with the drunken toast.

Kaia grins and gulps down her own pint, feeling a warmth bloom in her chest that has nothing to do with the alcohol. The night out is bittersweet, tainted slightly by the hollow ache of Hallie's absence. But as Adam slings an arm around her shoulders and crows about their killer teamwork in training, Kaia allows herself to forget for a moment that she'll be going home to an empty bed.

13

HALLIE

Over the following week after telling Kaia they had to put their careers before their feelings, Hallie watches with a mixture of awe and longing as the rookie seamlessly integrates herself into the fabric of her squad. Gone is the reckless loner who charged headfirst into any situation without a second thought. In her place is a team player, a confident and dependable firefighter who understands the importance of communication and trust.

During today's rescue simulation, Hallie finds herself transfixed by Kaia's performance. The rookie takes charge of coordinating her crew's movements, her voice steady and sure as she directs them through the maze of obstacles, and every one of the guys listens and obeys.

No snide remarks.

No disdainful side eyes.

Hallie can't help but feel a swell of pride as she listens to Kaia's calm, precise instructions. A leader in the making.

It's a stark contrast to the Kaia of mere weeks ago, the one who would have barreled ahead without a thought for her fellow firefighters. The one whose fellow recruits would rather knock her down a peg than listen to her strategies. Hallie knows she should be pleased by this development, should be satisfied that her strict approach to training protocol seems to finally have sunk in. But instead, she finds herself grappling with a fresh wave of sadness, a desperate yearning to close this alien distance between them and tell Kaia how proud she is.

How much she misses her.

The thought is like a punch to the gut, stealing the lieutenant's breath and making her eyes sting with threatening tears. She furiously blinks them back. She can't afford to let anyone see her wavering, least of all Kaia. Hallie had sacrificed everything there was between them to put both of their careers first. Like hell was she going to fall apart in the middle of the damn station.

But try as she might, Hallie can't convince herself to see Kaia as just another recruit. Every unspoken emotion is still there between them. It's in the charged silence that falls whenever they find themselves in their locker room at the same time. It's in the way their gaze lingers on each other when they think the other isn't looking.

And every night when she lies in bed alone and stares at the ceiling, Hallie can't help but wonder if Kaia is doing the same thing, thinking of her.

The next morning, as they're suiting up for a station-wide inspection, Hallie catches sight of Kaia in one of the locker room mirrors. The rookie's face is almost gaunt, dark circles blooming under her eyes as if she hasn't slept in days. But there's still that determined set to her jaw, that fire in her gaze that makes Hallie's heart pound.

Their eyes meet briefly in the glass, a thousand unspoken words hanging in the air between them. Kaia opens her mouth as if to say something, then seems to think better of it. She drops her gaze and busies herself with buttoning her turnout gear.

Hallie sighs, that heavy weight now permanently sitting on her chest as she watches Kaia turn and march out. The lieutenant's mind swirls with all the things she thought the rookie might have been about to say. Perhaps that she hoped Hallie thought better of her, now that she was throwing everything she had into gelling with her team. Perhaps that she hoped Hallie might have reconsidered ending their relationship, now that Kaia was proving that she could put aside her emotions and live up to her lieutenant's exacting standards.

But it's not that simple, Hallie thinks to herself, her fingers fumbling over the fastenings on her own uniform. Even Kaia becoming the best firefighter this station has ever trained, it wouldn't change that fact that their relationship could irrevocably damage both of their reputations if it ever became public knowledge.

The thought of losing her hard-earned position, of watching her dreams of making captain crumble to ashes, is enough to make Hallie's resolve harden again in her gut. She's worked too hard to get where she is, poured her blood, sweat, and tears into earning the respect of her peers and superiors alike. She could never risk all of that just for a shot at love.

And it was her fault that she let both of them get their hopes up in the first place.

She knows this with every fiber of her being. So why can't her aching heart get the message?

The uncertainty gnaws at her, a constant pain in her chest that grows more insistent with each passing day. Hallie finds herself just going through the motions, her mind always a million miles away even as she barks orders and runs drills with mechanical precision.

By the time the weekend arrives again, the stoic lieutenant is a shell of her former self. While packing up her gear and striding out to her car, Hallie's thoughts are once again consumed by the memory of Kaia's laughter. The phantom warmth of her skin. The way she sometimes seems to hold her breath right when she's on the edge of coming.

The sun is setting over the city as Hallie drives home, painting the sky in the same vivid streaks of orange and pink that it had the night they'd watched it together from her favorite ridge. But Hallie doesn't even notice its beauty tonight. She just absentmindedly crawls through the Friday night traffic, trying and failing to remember a time when she didn't miss Kaia's lips.

Eventually pulling into the parking lot for her

apartment complex and having no idea how she'd got there, Hallie throws her head back against her seat.

"Enough is enough, Lieutenant," she mutters to herself. "You have to get a fucking grip."

The following morning, she packs a bag and decides to take a train out of the city. It's time she unpacked everything she was feeling with the two people she trusts most in the world.

Less than two hours later, Hallie strolls up the front path of a cozy two-story house she knows better than any other house on Earth. She raises her hand to knock on the door, but before her knuckles can even make contact, it swings open to reveal her father's beaming face.

"Hallie-Pallie!" he exclaims, his eyes crinkling at the corners before he pulls her into a tight hug. "What a wonderful surprise! Your mom and I were just sitting down to breakfast. Come on in, there's plenty to go around."

Hallie feels some of the tension drain from her shoulders immediately as she steps into the familiar warmth of her childhood home. The mouthwatering aroma of her mother's famous blueberry pancakes wafts from the kitchen.

"Thanks, Pop," she murmurs, her voice thick

with emotion. "I'm sorry for not calling ahead. I just... I needed to see you."

Her father's brow furrows a little in concern as he no doubt spots the weariness etched into Hallie's features. He doesn't comment though, just gently takes her arm, leading her into the kitchen where her mother is setting the table.

"You never have to apologize for coming home, Hallie," he says firmly, guiding her into a chair. "Now, why don't you tell us what's on your mind while we eat? You look like you've got the weight of the world on your shoulders."

Hallie takes a shuddering breath, suddenly overwhelmed by the sheer magnitude of everything she's been grappling with. Her mother sets a loaded plate in front of her, the food a welcome distraction as her parents take their seats across the table.

"I'm just... I don't know where to start," Hallie admits at last, her voice barely above a whisper. "I guess... I was seeing someone. A rookie at the station. Kaia. And I think... I think I'm in love with her."

Hallie's father leans back in his chair, his expression thoughtful as he takes in her words. "In love, huh? That's a big deal, Hallie-Pallie. So, what's the drama?"

"The problem is that I'm her lieutenant," Hallie says slowly, pushing her food around her plate. "If anyone found out about us, it could ruin both our careers. I've worked so hard to get where I am, Pop. I'm scared of risking it all."

He nods, his eyes filled with understanding. "I can see why you're worried. Your position is important to you, and it should be. But let me ask you this—when you picture your future, what do you see? Is it a life filled with nothing but work? Or is it a life shared with someone you love?"

Hallie blinks back the creeping sting of tears, her father's words make it sound so simple. She thinks of all the long, lonely nights she's spent pouring over training protocols and incident reports. Of the emptiness that seems to fill her chest whenever she imagines a future without someone by her side.

"I see Kaia," she whispers, her voice cracking with emotion. "I wanted us to build a life together. But I screwed it up, Pop. I ran away. What if I can't balance my career and a relationship?"

He reaches across the table, his weathered hand covering hers with a gentle squeeze. "No one ever said it would be easy, Hallie. But you've never been one to back down from a challenge. If you love this girl, really love her, then you owe it to yourself to fight for her."

When her mom reaches out to place her own hand on top of theirs, Hallie feels something break open inside her chest, a dam of pent-up emotion flooding her veins.

"You're right," Hallie says softly, a sense of calm determination settling over her. "I can't let her go and just assume I'll get another chance down the line. She's here now, and she deserves to be fought for."

Her parents both smile, pride shining in their eyes as they each give her hand a final squeeze. "That's my girl," her mom says gently. "Now, finish your breakfast and tell us all about this Kaia. I want all the details."

Hallie huffs a small laugh, an easy smile tugging at the corners of her mouth as she tucks into her meal with renewed appetite. For the first time in weeks, she feels a glimmer of hope. A sense that maybe, just maybe, she can have the life her parents have after all.

Later that afternoon, Hallie decides to cut her trip home short and boards the train back to the city, her stomach fluttering with nervous anticipation. She barely notices the sparse towns and arid desert passing her by. This time round, her mind is swirling with all the things she wants to say to Kaia.

I'm sorry. I was wrong. I miss you. Please give me another chance.

The words play on a loop in her mind as the train winds its way back to the city, the gentle rocking of the carriage doing little to soothe her fraying nerves. She pulls out her phone, her thumb hovering over Kaia's contact as she tries to summon the courage to take the first step.

Come on, Hunter. You've got this.

Taking a deep breath, Hallie begins to type, her fingers trembling slightly as she pours her heart out onto the screen. She tries to ignore the previous message she sent. The cold dismissal that Kaia never responded to. Hallie couldn't blame her.

I need to see you.

My train gets in at 3.

Can I come over?

Hallie's thumb hovers over the send button, her blood pounding in her ears as she reads and re-reads the words. Should she say more? She would rather say everything she wants to in person. But will Kaia even respond?

With a final, shaky exhale, Hallie hits send, watching as the message disappears into the ether. All she can do now is hope that Kaia will at least give her a chance to speak what's on her mind. The rest is out of her hands.

Hallie leans back in her seat, her eyes drifting closed as she tries to calm her racing heart. She pictures Kaia's stunning face, the way her eyes crinkle at the corners when she laughs, the way her unruly dark curls splay over her pillow as she sleeps. She imagines a future filled with lazy Sunday mornings and late-night movies, of coming home after a grueling shift and having someone who understands exactly how it is. Who went through it right by her side.

The thought brings a smile to Hallie's face, a warmth blooming in her chest that chases away the lingering chill of doubt. She's ready, ready to fight for the woman she loves, ready to build a life together that's full of endless possibilities. Even if she never makes captain, she'll have everything she needs in life to be totally content. To be happy.

Suddenly, deafening screech rips through the

air. The train lurches violently, throwing her from her seat and sending her crashing to the floor.

Chaos erupts around her, a cacophony of screams and shattering glass filling the carriage as the world tilts on its axis. Hallie feels a searing pain explode behind her eyes as her head slams against the metal edge of a tray table, the force of the impact sending white dots across her vision.

She tries to push herself up, the emergency responder in her trying to make sense of the pandemonium unfolding all around, but her limbs refuse to cooperate. She can feel a warm, sticky wetness trickling down the side of her face, the coppery scent of blood filling her nostrils as her eyelids start to feel as heavy as lead.

No... Kaia. I have to get to Kaia.

It's the last thought that flickers through Hallie's mind before the darkness claims her, dragging her from consciousness even as she fights to cling on.

14

KAIA

Kaia paces the length of her apartment, her heart hammering against her ribcage with a dizzying mix of excitement and nerves. Hallie's message plays on a loop in her mind, each word a tantalizing promise.

I need to see you. Can I come over?

The text had sent a jolt of electricity through Kaia's veins when she'd first seen Hallie's name pop up on the screen, her hands shaking so badly could barely make out the letters at first. After weeks of agonizing silence, of trying to convince herself that she could live without Hallie's touch, her laughter, her fierce passion, Hallie had finally reached out. She wants to talk.

Just as she's buttoning a clean shirt with trembling hands, Kaia's phone buzzes with an incoming call. Her heart leaps into her throat, a giddy smile already tugging at her lips as she reaches for her back pocket.

But the smile fades as quickly as it had appeared as Kaia registers the caller ID. It's not Hallie, it's the station. Frowning, Kaia swipes to answer, her stomach already twisting with unease.

"Montgomery," she says, her voice coming out clipped and tense.

"Kaia, it's Captain Hewitt. We have a major emergency—all personnel are being called in. Get to the station as soon as you can."

Kaia feels the blood drain from her face, her heart stuttering to a halt in her chest. What could be so extreme that everyone off duty was being called in to help? The memory of the burning resort tower flickers behind her eyelids, making her wince. They haven't faced any major emergencies since, and Kaia hadn't realized until now how much that horrifying experience had stuck with her.

"I'll be right there," Kaia manages to choke out, already reaching for her discarded uniform. But even as Kaia tries to rationalize away the icy fear gripping her lungs, she can't shake the sinking feeling that something is very, very wrong.

With fumbling fingers, she dials Hallie's number as she rushes out the door, praying with every fiber of her being that the lieutenant will pick up. She could use some strong words of encouragement right now.

But the call goes straight to voicemail, Hallie's crisp tone echoing in Kaia's ear like a cruel taunt. Kaia fights to calm her racing heart as she sprints down the stairs of her building, her mind spinning with worst-case scenarios.

This is what you're trained for, Kaia. Calm the fuck down.

By the time Kaia screeches into the fire station's parking lot, her heart is pounding so hard she feels like it might burst from her ribcage. Hallie still hasn't answered her phone.

She leaps from her car and races inside, drinking in the controlled chaos erupting around her as her fellow firefighters rush to gear up and head out.

In the briefing room, Captain Hewitt stands at the front, his face grim as he details the situation.

"Listen up, everyone. We have a big job on our hands. Two passenger trains have collided head-

on just outside the city limits. Initial reports indi-
cate a signaling malfunction is to blame. We're
looking at massive casualties and a highly unstable
scene. Squads from Stations 1, 2, 5 and 7 are
already on site."

Kaia suddenly feels like the floor has dropped
out from under her, her vision swimming as the
captain's words wash over her in a dull roar.

Train collision. Massive casualties.

Hallie was on a train. Hallie isn't answering her
phone.

Kaia barely hears the rest of the short briefing,
her mind stuck in a loop of paralyzing terror. She
tries to focus on the rescue logistics, on the adren-
aline-fueled energy of her crewmates as they
prepare to head into the fray. But all she can think
about is Hallie.

Hallie, who should be here with them all,
barking orders and radiating that unwavering
confidence that always makes Kaia feel like they
can conquer anything as a team.

Hallie, who could be bleeding out in the
twisted wreckage of a train car right now, alone
and afraid and slipping away with every passing
second.

As everyone starts to move out, Kaia grabs Art

by the elbow. "Have you heard from Hallie? She was on a train this afternoon. She texted me earlier, but now she's not answering and I'm—"

Kaia's voice cracks, the words sticking in her throat like shards of glass. Art's eyes widen with dawning realization, his brow furrowing as he shakes his head.

"I haven't heard from her. Shit, Kaia... You don't think...?"

He doesn't finish the question, but he doesn't need to. The same icy dread is written all over his face.

Kaia swallows hard, steeling herself against the wave of emotion threatening to drown her. She can't fall apart right now. Hallie needs her to be strong, to be the firefighter she's trained her to be.

"We have to get out there," Kaia says, her voice low and fierce. "Maybe she's not there. Maybe her phone just died."

Art nods grimly, his jaw tight with resolve. Together, they rush to join their crew, the weight of their shared fear hanging heavy in the air between them.

The scene at the crash site is like something out of a nightmare. Crumpled carriages lie along the tracks, the acrid smell of smoke and spilled diesel fuel burning Kaia's nostrils. Everywhere she looks, she sees injured passengers stumbling from the wreckage, their faces streaked with blood and soot.

But as Kaia surveys the devastation, her blood pounding in her ears, there's only one face she's desperate to find. The same face she's also praying she doesn't see.

Where are you, Hallie?

Kaia forces herself to take a deep breath, to slip into the focused headspace she's been trained to adopt. She can't afford to let her panic consume her, not when there are lives at stake. With a herculean effort, she pushes thoughts of Hallie to the back of her mind and springs into action alongside her squad.

The next few hours pass in a blur of adrenaline and sweat as seemingly every emergency responder in the city works tirelessly to extract victims from the mangled train cars. Kaia crawls through jagged openings and climbs over upturned seats, her heart in her throat with every new survivor she discovers.

None of them are Hallie.

As Kaia carries another barely conscious victim into a waiting ambulance, her muscles screaming with fatigue, she overhears a pair of paramedics talking in low, urgent tones.

"...Hunter, I think. Blunt force trauma to the head, nasty laceration to the thigh..."

Kaia's legs nearly give out from under her, her vision darkening as the paramedic's words sink in like poison darts.

She deposits her charge on a gurney and whirls around, grabbing the arm of the nearest paramedic with a white-knuckled grip.

"The casualty you just mentioned. Hunter. Do you mean Hallie Hunter? The lieutenant from Fire Station 3?" Kaia demands, her voice shaking with barely restrained panic.

"I... I don't know. She was pretty banged up, but it looked like her."

Kaia's stomach plummets, a wave of dizzying nausea crashing over her. She fumbles for her radio, her voice cracking as she calls for the captain.

"Captain Hewitt, do you have eyes on Lieutenant Hunter? I heard... I heard the paramedics picked up someone who looked like Hallie."

There's a pause on the other end of the line, an agonizing stretch of static that seems to last an eternity.

Then, the captain's voice crackles through, heavy with grim resignation.

"Montgomery... Yes, Hunter's been located. She was transported to a hospital in critical condition maybe ten minutes ago. Montgomery... I have to warn you... it doesn't look good."

The ground seems to drop out from beneath Kaia's feet. She staggers back a step, her radio almost slipping from her trembling fingers.

This can't be happening. This can't be real. She was coming back to me.

Kaia stands frozen amidst the ongoing chaos, her mind reeling as she tries to process the captain's words. Every instinct in her body is screaming at her to run, to race to the hospital and find Hallie, to hold her hand and beg her to stay alive.

But she's torn, a fierce sense of duty warring with the desperate need in her chest. She knows Hallie would want her to stay focused on the rescue, to put the needs of the citizens before her own. It's what she's trained for, what Hallie has drilled into each and every rookie from day one.

Kaia looks around slowly at the still-smoldering wreckage. It's impossible to know at this point how many more survivors need to be pulled out.

But then, Captain Hewitt's voice crackles through the radio again, this time softer, almost soothing.

"Montgomery, listen to me. I think I know what Lieutenant Hunter means to you. I've had my suspicions for a while now, and it's okay. You can go to her. We'll handle things here."

Kaia's eyes well with tears, her throat tightening with a surge of gratitude and relief. But still, she hesitates.

"But Hallie... she would want me to stay," she whispers, more to herself than to the captain. "She would put the job first, no matter what."

Beside her, Richards appears and places a gentle hand on her shoulder, his expression understanding.

"Kaia, you should go," he says gently. "We've got this. Hunter would do the same for you, and you know it."

"Thank you," Kaia mumbles, seizing Adam in a quick, fierce hug before sprinting towards the line of waiting ambulances. She spots one that's about to leave, two paramedics closing the rear doors while another leaps into the driver's seat.

"Wait!" Kaia cries out, waving her arms frantically. "I need to come with you. My... my partner, she was taken in on another rig."

The paramedic in the front snaps his head up, spotting Kaia and jerking his chin towards the passenger seat, a silent invitation. Kaia scrambles into the ambulance, her heart lodged in her throat as she fastens her seatbelt with shaking hands.

As the ambulance peels away from the horrifying scene, sirens wailing, Kaia closes her eyes and sends up a desperate prayer.

"Hold on, Hallie," she whispers. "Just hold on for me. I'm coming."

She presses her forehead against the cool glass of the window, watching the city blur past through a haze of tears.

15

HALLIE

The first moment Hallie becomes aware feels like kicking up from the murky depths of a deep ocean. The next thing she registers is a dull, throbbing ache behind her eyes, as if her skull is being squeezed in a vise. She tries to blink, but her eyelids are heavy and uncooperative, as a steady beeping filters in through the fringe of her awareness.

Where am I? What the fuck happened?

Fragments of memory flicker behind her closed lids—the gentle rocking of the train, the buzz of anticipation as she typed out a text to Kaia. And then... chaos. A searing pain exploding in her head before everything went black.

Hallie's eyes flutter open as she claws her way

back to full consciousness, her heart monitor spiking with the sudden surge of adrenaline. She squints against harsh fluorescent lights, her surroundings gradually coming into focus. Sterile white walls, the sharp smell of antiseptic, a tangle of wires and tubes snaking from her arms.

The hospital. I must be in the hospital.

As Hallie is slowly piecing together her reality, she becomes aware of a warm pressure enveloping her hand. She glances down, her breath catching in her throat at the sight that greets her. Kaia is slumped in a chair beside the bed, her fingers wrapped around Hallie's, her head resting on the edge of the mattress as if she'd fallen asleep keeping vigil.

With her other, slightly trembling hand, Hallie reaches out to brush a stray curl from Kaia's forehead, instantly calmed by the familiar feel of her soft skin. Kaia stirs at the touch, her brow furrowing slightly before her eyes blink open. For a moment, she seems disoriented, head turning slowly as she takes in her surroundings. But then her gaze lands on Hallie, and her entire face transforms.

"Hallie," she breathes, her voice rough with sleep. "You're awake."

Tears are already welling in Kaia's eyes as she sits up, her grip tightening on Hallie's hand as if she's scared that Hallie will slip away again if she lets go. Hallie feels her own eyes start to burn, her throat constricting around the rising pressure of everything she wants to say.

"Kaia, I..." she starts, but her voice cracks, splintering around the rawness left by her ordeal. She swallows hard, trying again. "I'm so sorry, baby. I have some more groveling to do."

Kaia shakes her head, a watery smile tugging at her lips. "No, you don't. I'm the one who should be apologizing."

She leans in, pressing her forehead to Hallie's, and for a moment, the rest of the world falls away. There's no hospital, no beeping monitors, no aches or pains. There's just the two of them, breathing each other in, savoring the closeness they've gone without for too long.

When Kaia pulls back to wipe a stray tear from Hallie's cheek, the lieutenant notices the other figures sitting quietly on the other side of the room.

"Mom? Pop?" she croaks, her eyes widening in disbelief. "Gavin? What are you doing here?"

Her father steps forward, his weathered face

etched with a mix of worry and relief. He looks like he hasn't slept in days, his usually tidy hair disheveled and his clothes rumpled. Gavin is still in his uniform; he must have come straight from a shift at his own station.

"We came as soon as we heard about the crash, Hallie-Pallie," Pop says, approaching her bed. "It was a little touch and go for a while there."

When he reaches her side, he raises a large hand to rest on Hallie's shoulder with a gentleness that belies his size. Hallie leans into the touch, feeling some of the tension drain from her body at the comforting warmth of her family's presence.

"Thank you for coming," she whispers, a single tear slipping down her cheek. "I'm sorry it had to be under such shitty circumstances, but I guess I should introduce you to Kaia."

Pop shakes his head, a smile tugging at his lips. "You have nothing to apologize for, my love. We're just grateful you're okay."

He glances at Kaia, his eyes twinkling with something that looks a little like mischief. "And we've already been getting to know this lovely young lady while we waited for you to wake up. She's been filling us in on all your heroic escapades together."

Hallie feels a blush creep up her neck, her gaze darting to Kaia, who is gazing back at Pop with warm affection.

"Oh really?" Hallie asks, a hint of playfulness creeping into her tone. "And what kind of tales has she been spinning? Did she tell you what a pain in the ass she can be?"

Kaia's dark eyes snap to Hallie's, glinting with humor. "I only told them the truth, Lieutenant. That you're the bravest, most badass firefighter this city has ever seen. I left out the parts where I wasn't on my best behavior."

Hallie chuckles, warmth blooming in her chest at the admiration in Kaia's voice. But the laughter quickly turns into a cough, her ribs soon aching with the effort. Kaia immediately reaches for the cup of water on the nightstand, guiding the straw to Hallie's lips with a tenderness that makes her heart clench.

As she sips the cool liquid, Hallie catches her mom's eye over the rim of the cup. Her mother gives her a small nod, a silent acknowledgment passing between them.

"We'll give the two of you a minute," she says softly, jerking his head towards the door. "Come on, Sandy, let's go see if we can track down Hallie's doctor. And maybe some coffee while we're at it."

Pop nods, giving Hallie's shoulder a gentle squeeze before following her mom and Gavin out of the room. As the door clicks shut behind them, Hallie turns back to Kaia, her heart racing with sudden nerves.

This is the moment she's been both dreading and longing for in equal measure. The chance to finally say the words that have been burning on the tip of her tongue for weeks.

But before she can even open her mouth, Kaia beats her to it.

"I thought I lost you," she whispers, her voice cracking as fresh tears spill down her cheeks. "When I heard about the crash, and then you weren't answering your phone... I've never been so scared in my life."

Hallie feels her own eyes well up, the raw anguish in Kaia's voice piercing her already struggling lungs. She brings their joined hands to her lips, pressing a kiss to Kaia's knuckles.

"I'm so sorry, baby," she murmurs. "It shouldn't have taken me so long to reach out to you. If I had come to my senses sooner, I wouldn't have even been on that train. I shouldn't have needed my parents to help me see..."

She trails off, suddenly unsure how to put into words everything that she feels for this remarkable woman. But Kaia just smiles, a soft, knowing smile that makes Hallie forget what she was trying to say.

"I know," Kaia breathes, her thumb stroking over the back of Hallie's hand. "Your dad kind of let it slip while we were sitting with you. He said you had gone to see them."

Hallie feels a blush creep across her cheeks, a sheepish grin tugging at her lips. "Ah, so he filled you in on all that, huh? I guess that saves me the trouble of trying to remember the speech I had all planned out."

Kaia leans in closer, her breath ghosting over Hallie's face as she asks, "And what exactly were you planning to say to me, Lieutenant Hunter?"

Hallie takes a deep inhale, her heart hammering against her ribcage as she gazes into Kaia's warm, expectant eyes.

"I was going to say that I'm sorry," she begins. "For being so stubborn, for pushing you away when all I wanted was to pull you closer. I thought I was protecting us both, but I was just afraid. Of how much you mean to me, of how badly I wanted to risk everything just to be with you."

Kaia's dark eyes widen, her lips parting in surprise as Hallie's words tumble out. But she doesn't interrupt, just squeezes Hallie's hand in silent encouragement to continue.

Emboldened by the feeling of finally laying out her true feelings, Hallie pushes on.

"I love you, Kaia. I'm so desperately, hopelessly in love with you. And I'm sorry it took me so long to realize that my career means nothing to me if I don't have you to come home to."

The tears are streaming freely down Kaia's face now, but she's smiling, a breathtaking, radiant smile that Hallie has missed so much.

"I love you too, Hallie," she whispers. "And I'm so sorry for being reckless, for putting you in a position where you felt like you couldn't count on me. I only ever wanted to make you proud, but I hid behind my own ego for way too long."

Hallie finds herself too overwhelmed with emotion to respond. She sighs, tilting her chin up to capture Kaia's lips in a soft, tender kiss. It's a kiss full of promises, of forgiveness, of a love that neither of them is holding back any longer.

When they finally part, both slightly breathless, Kaia rests her head on Hallie's shoulder, careful not to jostle any of the wires or tubes. For a long moment, they just breathe each other in, savoring the quiet intimacy they've gone too long without sharing.

Kaia is the one to eventually break the silence, raising her head with a slightly guilty expression. "Oh, I almost forgot. Captain Hewitt sends his well wishes. I think he's known about us for a while."

Hallie's eyes widen, a spark of anxiety igniting in her chest. "He has? What did he say to you?"

Kaia just shrugs, a small smirk playing at the corner of her mouth. "Nothing much. But when he gave me permission to leave the scene to be with you, he kinda implied that he thought something was going on between us. I don't think we're going to be fired the minute we walk back into the station."

Relief washes over Hallie like a cooling balm. "Well, that's one less thing to worry about, I guess. Can't wait to have that awkward chat with him."

Kaia giggles, the sound bright and soothing, and Hallie feels her own lips curve into a grin. God, she's missed that sound. Missed the way Kaia's whole face lights up when she laughs, when her eyes crinkle at the corners and her nose scrunches up in that adorable way.

A soft knock at the door distracts her from her smitten staring, and Hallie looks up to see her parents and brother poking their heads in, warm grins spreading across their faces as they take in the scene they've walked in on.

"Well, look what we have here," Mom chuckles, her eyes twinkling with mirth as she steps into the room. "Seems like you two have sorted a few things out."

Hallie feels a blush heat her face, but she can't help the smile that's starting to ache across her cheeks. "Yeah, Mom. I think we might have."

Gavin strides over to the bed, clapping Kaia on the shoulder. "Welcome to the family, Kaia. I hope you can handle a bunch more Hunters giving you grief. Though Hallie is definitely the difficult one, so I'm sure you'll put up with the rest of us just fine."

Kaia laughs, leaning into the touch with an ease that makes Hallie's heart swell. "Yeah, I think I can handle it."

As her family settles in around her, their chatter and laughter filling the sterile hospital room with warmth and love, Hallie catches Kaia's eye across the bed.

"I love you," she whispers, relishing the feeling of finally being able to share what took her so long to realize.

Kaia leans down to capture Hallie's lips with her own. "I love you too," she murmurs. "Now, tell your brother about that time I beat your ass at suicide sprints. He doesn't believe I outran you."

EPILOGUE
HALLIE

Hallie strides through the familiar doors of Fire Station 3, her chest swelling with pride and anticipation as she returns to work after months of grueling recovery. Kaia had been there every step of the way, of course. The lieutenant smiles at the thought of her sexy, live-in nurse, of the gentle pressure of Kaia's hands guiding Hallie through physical therapy exercises, the soft brush of her lips against Hallie's forehead as she soothed her through the pain and frustration.

When she eventually pauses outside the captain's office door, Hallie takes a deep breath to center herself before raising her fist to knock. The gruff, "Come in!" that answers sends a jolt down her spine, the nerves creeping in. She has spent weeks being anxious about this first meeting back at work, knowing that Captain Hewitt had suspected she and Kaia had been involved for a while before the train crash.

As Hallie enters the office, her breath catches in surprise to find not only Captain Hewitt but also the district fire chief, Curt Walters, waiting for her. She feels her pulse quicken, palms growing damp as she tries to read their stoic expressions. This is highly unusual.

"Lieutenant Hunter," the Chief Walters greets her, a warm smile crinkling the corners of his eyes. "Damn good to see you back. Have a seat."

Hallie sinks into a chair, her mind racing with possibilities—good and bad—as Hewitt leans forward, hands clasped on his desk.

"Hunter, we asked you here today because, frankly, we've been blown away by the caliber of firefighters your Probationary Field Training program has produced." The captain's voice is filled with unabashed admiration, making Hallie's cheeks warm.

Chief Walters nods vigorously, his gaze intent on Hallie's face. "I've been keeping tabs on this rookie class. Their teamwork, discipline, technical skills—it's outstanding on all fronts. All thanks to your formidable leadership."

Hallie blinks rapidly, overwhelmed by the unexpected praise. She feels a lump form in her throat, this is the validation she's worked so tirelessly for all these years.

"Thank you," she manages, fighting to keep her voice steady. "I gave it everything I had."

A beat of silence follows as the chief exchanges a loaded glance with Hewitt. Hallie barely remembers to take a breath, apprehension bearing down on her in the dimly lit office.

"Well, Hunter," Chief Walters begins, leaning forward in his seat, "we didn't just call you in here to blow smoke up your ass. We have an opportunity we think you're ready for, if you want it."

Hallie's blood is roaring in her ears, her mind tripping over itself trying to grasp what the chief might be saying.

Captain Hewitt's face splits into a wide grin. "Congratulations, Captain Hunter. The promotion is yours; you've damn well earned it."

The world seems to stop spinning for a moment, Hallie's breath seizing in her lungs as the title registers.

Captain Hunter.

After years of pouring her blood, sweat, and tears into this department, into this job. After fighting tooth and nail to prove her worth in a constant swarm of skeptical men... This is really happening.

Speechless, all Hallie can do is nod, a disbelieving laugh bubbling up from her chest as Hewitt and Chief Walters both chuckle at her stunned reaction.

"Now, normally we'd be falling over ourselves to keep a leader of your reputation in this district," Fire Chief Walters continues, his expression turning pensive. "I've got open positions across multiple departments that would kill to have you."

He leans forward then, an almost conspiratorial gleam in his eye that sets Hallie's brain buzzing with curiosity. "But something tells me you might be interested in another opportunity, a little further afield."

Hallie tilts her head, intrigue warring with the elation still simmering in her veins. "Further afield, Sir?"

The chief shares another meaningful look with Hewitt, "Have you heard of Phoenix Ridge? Busy town, about an hour across the state line."

Hallie shakes her head, her brows furrowing as

she tries to place the name. It's not ringing any bells. Why would the chief be talking about a job in another state when he just said there are open captain positions closer to home?

The chief's grin widens. "Well, turns out they've got a real trailblazing fire department over there. First in the country to be all female, top to bottom."

Hallie thinks her heart might actually have stopped in her chest. An all-female department? She'd never heard of such a thing.

"Their chief has caught wind of your achievements through the grapevine," Chief Walters continues. "She thinks you'd make a great addition to the department, if you're interested."

Hallie sinks back in her chair, mind reeling as she tries to wrap her head around the whole thing. To have the opportunity to lead a team of women who understand the challenges and triumphs of making it in this field. To shape the future of a department that values their skill and dedication above all else. She'd pack a bag right this minute.

A shuddering breath escapes Hallie's lips, tears pricking at the corners of her eyes as she meets the chief's patient gaze. "I'm definitely interested, Sir," she manages, voice thick with barely restrained emotion. "This... this sounds like an incredible opportunity."

Captain Hewitt claps his hands together. "You deserve it, Hunter. You've more than earned a command of your own. You'll be sorely missed, but I know you'll do great things over there. Montgomery too, of course."

Chief Walters nods. "I'll put you in touch with the Phoenix Ridge brass. If you decide it's the right move for you, just say the word and the job is yours."

Hallie rises on shaky legs, her heart fuller than she ever thought possible as she shakes the chief's hand, then Hewitt's. She thanks them profusely, practically floating out of the office on a cloud of euphoria.

That evening, Hallie sits on the couch, her thoughts a million miles away as she waits for Kaia to get home from a call out. She chuckles at the memory of getting her text as she left the station.

You can head home without me.

I have to go save another damn cat.

Art says he'll get me a badge when I reach double digits.

The jingle of keys in the lock snaps her out of her musing, and she looks up just in time to see

Kaia burst through the door, an easy smile on her face.

"Hey, you, how was your first day back?" Kaia asks, making a beeline for Hallie and pulling her into a fierce kiss. "I missed you out there, could have used your cat-charming abilities."

Hallie smiles against Kaia's lips, savoring the sweet familiarity of her touch before pulling back slightly, her expression turning serious.

"It was good. Really good, actually," she begins, taking Kaia's hands in her own. "I need to talk to you about something pretty big."

Kaia's brow furrows as she settles onto the couch. "What's going on? Is everything okay?"

Hallie takes a deep breath, searching for the right words to convey the sheer magnitude of what happened in her meeting this morning. Slowly, haltingly, she recounts her conversation with Chief Walters and Hewitt, watching as Kaia's expression morphs from worry to shock to pure joy.

"Captain Hunter!" Kaia exclaims, leaping to her feet and pulling Hallie up with her, into a bone-crushing hug. "Fuck, I'm so proud of you! You deserve this more than anyone."

Hallie laughs, her heart full to bursting as she clings to Kaia, relishing the feeling of her strong arms wrapped around her. "Thanks, baby. But there's more..."

She pulls back slightly, cupping Kaia's face in her hands as she explains the chief's recommendation of the captain position at the Phoenix Ridge Fire Department. As she speaks, Hallie watches Kaia's face closely, trying to gauge her reaction as the offer dawns on her. To her surprise, Kaia's eyes light up with what looks like yearning, a wistful smile playing at the corners of her lips.

"An all-female department? Are you kidding?" Kaia eventually responds, her voice soft with wonder. "Hallie, that sounds like a dream come true."

Hallie barely gives herself a second to hope before double checking that Kaia's actually on board with the whole idea. "You really think so? It would be a big change, moving to a new town, joining a new station. I know you've only just started to find your groove with the crew here..."

But Kaia is already shaking her head. "Babe, I love our squad. I really do. But if I'm being honest... the idea of spending the rest of my career fighting to compete with men who will always see me as lesser? That sounds more exhausting than it's worth."

Hallie can't help but chuckle, she knows that feeling perhaps better than anyone.

"I want to be judged on my skills, my dedication. Not my gender," Kaia continues. "If you really want this, if you think it could be a good move for us, then I'm all in."

Hallie feels the threat of tears prick at her eyes, emotion welling up in her throat as Kaia's words sink in. Her unwavering support. The willingness to uproot her life and start anew. Hallie never thought she could be so lucky to have such a partner.

"I love you so much," she whispers fiercely, pulling Kaia in for a searing kiss that leaves them both breathless. "Let's do it. Let's start over somewhere new, you and me."

As the night wears on and they start to make plans, Hallie feels a sense of overwhelming peace settle deep in her bones. She thinks of how far they've come, from that first charged meeting in the station to the heartbreak and catastrophe they've had to overcome to get here.

Curled up in bed later that night, Kaia's head resting on her chest, Hallie lets her mind wander to the future that stretches out before them both. She imagines they might have a life like her parents, madly in love and fiercely dedicated to their careers until the day they decide to retire together.

As she drifts off to sleep, Hallie sends up a silent prayer of gratitude for the twists and turns of fate that have led them to this moment. For the love that has seen them through the darkest of times, and the bright future that awaits them on the other side.

And as Hallie tightens her arms around Kaia, breathing in the sweet scent of her wild curls, she knows that there is nowhere else she would rather be. No one else she would rather face the world with.

This is their next chapter, and Hallie can't wait to see where it leads them. Together.

WHAT'S NEXT?

Follow on with the Phoenix Ridge Fire Series and check out book 2: mybook.to/PRF2

If you liked Hallie and Kaia's story, I think you will love it!

FREE BOOK

I really hope you enjoyed this story. I loved writing it.

I'd love for you to get my FREE book- Her Boss- by joining my mailing list. On my mailing list you can be the first to find out about free or discounted books or new releases and get short sexy stories for free! Just click on the following link or type into your web browser: https://BookHip.com/MNVVPBP

Meg has had a huge crush on her hot older boss for

some time now. Could it be possible that her crush is reciprocated? https://BookHip.com/MNVVPBP

Printed in Great Britain
by Amazon

54783227R00115